NIGHT OWL

VEIL OF SHADOWS

BOOK SIX

M. R. PRITCHARD

Paperback ISBN: 978-1-957709-41-3

For the ones who stay up late arguing with their Demons and thinking about monsters and happy endings.

You can't silence this heartbeat.

Meg didn't want the heartbeat in her womb or the constant threat to her friends. She decides it's best to disappear. Meg runs to the Earthen plane to hide and plan her next step. While lighting strikes and dark hungers keep her running, a mysterious man seems a little too helpful. Will Meg destroy the one man who will follow her through hell and high water?

TURNED TO GRAY

MEG

The warm body next to me shifts, dragging the sheet. I open my eyes. It's Skeele. Of course it's Skeele. It wouldn't be anyone else. He didn't leave after I fed. He was probably too tired. It's been weeks since dinner in the ballroom and things have been off between us. Not that they were ever really going well. He's still grumpy but does whatever I tell him. Every time I need him, he's there.

The aroma of coffee fills the room as a breeze blows through the open balcony doors. Noah left coffee and donuts. Not long ago I loved the smell. But today, it causes my stomach to lurch. I slide out of the bed and run to the bathroom.

"What?" Skeele asks, sitting up quickly, ready to fight.

I wave as I run, slam the bathroom door, lock it, and dry heave into the sink since there's no food in my stomach to puke up. I turn the water on high to hide the sounds. I don't want him to know. I don't want him to ask. From the corner of my eye, I watch the doorhandle to see if it moves, to see if he tries to follow me in here. I don't want to be caught purging my hopes and dreams into the sink.

It's nothing, I tell myself. *Just ate some bad burritos.* Burritos are never really bad though. I watch my distorted reflection in the sink plug. It could be worse. I could be broke and homeless and living on the Earthen plane. Yeah, that's it. I could be stuck never knowing that I was more than just a trailer-park girl in a small-town fighting like a rabid animal to live the American dream. I grab a towel and wipe my face. Look at me now.

I lean against the counter and press my face into the towel. *Look at me now.* I have fluffy towels, a proper bed, a kitchen with food, clothes that I didn't have to steal. Squeezing my cheeks, I swallow down the lump that's rising in my throat.

———

SKEELE

Skeele opened his eyes and lay still, listening to the sounds of Meg retching in the bathroom. Gnawing doubt and torment clawed at his heart. He gave himself to Meg, gave his body and his blood but he couldn't shake the persistent feeling that she despised him. She'd said it to his face enough times. His mind spun with uncertainty. The time they'd spent together in the darkest hours of the night seemed like a cruel illusion, tormenting him with false hope. He was sinking into a pit of self-doubt and despair. It had been hard to forget after his fight with the Archangels. He couldn't ignore their words.

Dirty pig, Disgusting Hellion, wretched dog.

Skeele stood and straightened the blankets. He collected his clothes, catching his reflection in the mirror. Shadows crossed his face. *I have pledged my life to her*, he thought, *why does she despise me? I make her physically ill. She can't even look at me.*

Skeele dressed quickly and left the room.

He walked through the halls of the castle within the burning caves. The pain of rejection would serve as fuel; he would remain loyal, a relentless warrior, a commander of unparalleled strength. He would ensure Meg's reign would be unchallenged, her enemies crushed. She could hate him, but he would forever remain loyal and serve. It was in his bloodline, his fate forever solidified in the stars of Hellsky. Meg could use him, that's what he was born and bred for. Serve the throne, nothing more.

Skeele was dizzy, his throat becoming drier with each step. He felt like he hadn't eaten in weeks. He tugged at the waist of his pants. They were looser than ever. He had fed Meg, but didn't take from her like before. Something internal warned him not to. He couldn't place the feeling, but he sensed she needed all the blood for herself. That wound on her arm wasn't healing and Skeele didn't want to risk her not being in full health.

He took one step down the winding stairs that led to the Hellion lair, and on the second step, something strange happened to his body. The fog in his brain intensified, he stumbled, then fell. Skeele rolled down the stairs like a tossed mannequin. He finally stopped at the first landing where the stairwell turned sharply. Dark red blood dripped into his eye, but he didn't care much because he passed out.

———

Meg

"I can't go on like this." I slap my hands on the table. "Last night I almost drained Skeele." I shake the memory and the fear away. "I could barely control myself. Klaus found him collapsed on the stairs this morning. I almost killed him. I can't do this." I run my hands through my hair and tug.

"He might understand," Teari suggests. "Maybe you should tell him. Then he can take proper precautions. He could carry extra bagged blood."

"No." I cut her off. "I want to know how to stop the puking. I want some control back–not that I ever had much, but this is worse. I feel like a dam ready to burst. Maybe it's the hormones. I don't know." I tug at my hair, ready to tear it out.

Teari holds up her finger. "I've been doing some research." She opens an old book. "I got this from the library in Babylon. There are actually a lot of historical books there."

"I don't really care." I lean back in my chair and set my feet on the table. I whistle a ho-hum trill. Just like the old days. I should stop that. "Just tell me how to get rid of this or survive it."

"Well, Meg," she shoves my feet off the table. "First you should remember that you are kind of like royalty now and you should have some manners." She flips through a few pages, and they crinkle like they've soaked in wine and dried in the sun. "You are not complete darkness." She reminds me. "You are half Angel. An Angel's gestation is about six months. You remember how quickly Nightingale had Thrush."

I nod.

"And Demons range from 18 to 20 months." She holds up a finger. "But you aren't full Demon."

"The father is."

"So there's that." She turns the crisp page of the book, and I make the mistake of looking at the pictures. Drawings in black and red of beastly looking creatures tearing apart vaginas and dead women laying on tables with their arms and legs askew and eyes deadened, wide open. So easily the pages could be illustrations from the movie The Shining with Demon babies hacking away at their mother's bodies just to make a grand entrance shouting "Here's Johnny!" amongst all the blood and gore.

"What the fuck, Teari?" I point to the picture. "Am I going to die giving birth to this monster?"

Teari slaps my hand away. "That's only what happens when they breed with humans." She clears her throat. "And we both know that you are not pure-blood human. You'll be fine. Remember Nightingale's delivery. You're a mixed blood, but the right kind of blood."

I cross my arms and stare at the ceiling. "So, if I don't get rid of this thing. I'm going to be a fat-ass for almost two years."

"You might grow in the belly, but you won't necessarily be a fat-ass, Meg. Maybe lay off the donuts." She closes the book. "You know you can't hide this from everyone. Some will tell you're pregnant immediately. They'll hear two heartbeats."

"Can the Hellions?" I ask, feeling like a jerk.

"Nope."

"Can the Angels?"

"Well, Archangels can. But regular Angels can't." She rubs her hands together.

"Does my father know?" I ask.

"I don't know," Teari says. "If he knows he has said nothing to me."

"I should probably get out of here before he sees me and finds out."

"Wait." Teari holds out her hands. "Let me just... check."

I grab her hands to stop her. "How about you just make it go away."

She elbows me and shoves my hands away. "I won't do that."

Her hands hover over my chest and slowly down to my belly. She frowns, a crease in her forehead. "Sit up straight."

I do, hoping for bad news.

One of her hands slides down my back. The other settles on my lower abdomen. She tips her head and closes her eyes. "You need more blood." She tips her head like she's trying to hear something. She moves her hands away and lifts the sleeve of my shirt to find the bandage still there. "This hasn't healed?"

"It's better than it used to be."

She pulls the gauze away revealing the deep cut. It's less deep than when it started but still oozes and aches every day. "Put the basilisk on it again. Every day for a week."

I sigh, grossed out.

"Do it, Meg." She hits my leg.

"Can you come do it?" I beg. "I like it better when you're there."

"I'm Gabriel's personal healer. I can't stay in Hell with you."

"I feel lost without you all," I confess to Teari. "Noah spends less and less time with me. He doesn't want me around Thrush. He just drops food and runs home to be with Nightingale and Thrush."

"You can't hate him for spending time with his family. Nightingale was dead, gone forever. Give him his time. He might not always have it." She wraps the gauze around my arm. "Go see Tukka. I told him how to use the basilisk."

"Fine." I sigh like a child. "So, you'll come for a weekend maybe?"

"Gabriel has me very busy here. We are rebuilding. Several Legion were injured in the Fast-Zombie War. I can't go."

"Fine. Be that way," I pout.

Poof. I return to Hell.

There's a loud knock on my door. I throw the covers back and get out of bed to answer it wearing the old flannel I woke up in that one day when I jumped off the balcony. I open the door. Skeele's there.

"You haven't eaten in three days." His tone is annoyed.

"I'm not hungry."

I try to close the door, but Skeele's arm stops it. His big hand grips the edge of the door, holding the lock.

He says something in Hellspeak. I think he's calling me a liar but he never says it in plain English so I can understand.

He pushes the door open. I back up as he enters the room and closes the door behind his back.

"Nice shirt." His eyes linger.

"Thanks. I found it laying around." I sigh, knowing that I was too lazy to button the whole thing. "You can go back to your life, whatever you had planned tonight. You don't need to be here."

My stomach growls loud and it echoes. I cover my face with my hands, feeling stupid.

"Is that so?" His eyes lower.

"You have nothing to do tonight?" I ask. "You don't have to be here."

He walks closer. "I have something to do and that is feed my queen."

I let out an awkward, breathy laugh. My queen. "I'm not really a queen."

"You're not a king." He reaches for the shirt and peeks inside. "Definitely a queen."

It's hard to push him away when he's this close. Even harder to ignore the quick movement of his hands as he slices his wrist and holds it against my mouth.

"That's rude," I say, tipping my head back.

"Did you want to pray first?" The corners of his lips rise. He knows better, I'm not one to pray before meals. I'm not one to pray ever.

I scowl, grab his wrist, and press it against my mouth. "Mmm." The noise escapes my throat as I drink. It's been too long. His blood tastes like champagne on my tongue; tart and sweet and bubbly. It's warm, like he just came from a hot shower or working out. Since he smells like wood smoke and pine, it must be the hot shower. I savor the smell, close my eyes, and take a deep breath in as I lap at the blood dripping from his wrist like it's a melting ice-cream cone. I was supposed to let him go, not latch onto him like this. He probably had plans tonight and here I am holding the monopoly on his time. It doesn't take long for the heat between my thighs to become unbearable.

Skeele sniffs the air. He tries to hide it, but I can tell. I think he can smell the bloodlust. Or maybe he can just smell me. I'm not sure and right now, I don't really care. He pushes me with his free hand, pressing against my stomach until the backs of my knees hit the mattress.

It all goes downhill from there. I promised to be better. I promised not to be selfish, to be cognizant and compassionate. I guess I'll try another day. Tonight is a complete loss. I take from Skeele everything he gives; his blood, his thickness and length, his Demon tongue. And I love every second.

———

I wake alone and not ready to puke. I get my coffee and donut from the table near the balcony and think about how cultured I've become. I haven't had an orange soda for breakfast in at least a month.

The sun seems too bright today, the chirping of the birds too loud. I wander to the back of the room and curl up in the club chair that's against the wall. It smells like Skeele. I guess it should since he spent enough time sitting in it and watching me come back to life.

Four sips in and I realize what a failure I was last night. I did nothing I promised. I rub my face. What the hell is wrong with me? Bad habits are hard to break, especially when they feel so good in the heat of the moment.

As I finish the coffee, I realize Skeele never took blood from me last night. I guess he's holding back. Maybe he's so fed up with me he can't bear to do it. Maybe it really turns him off. I've never asked. I thought he used to enjoy it. He absorbed my ability to travel at will. Maybe that's why.

———

Jed and Shay

The dead were wandering about quietly in the forest behind Jed and Shay. Sticks snapped, leaves rustled, moans interrupted Jed's teaching.

"Let's start with a warm-up exercise," Jed said, showing Shay how to stretch, twist, and tap her fingers into nimbleness.

Shay mimicked Jed's motions, her fingers moving faster and faster to keep up with him.

Jed watched her hands intensely. "That's good." His fingers moved in a rhythm only he seemed to know. He clucked his tongue lightly like a conductor so Shay could follow along to the beat. After three rounds he started with the first spell. Jed backed up in a circle, looking for the nearest walking corpse to practice on.

"That one," he jerked his chin to a dead man dragging his foot. "Like this." Jed's fingers danced as he cast a spell to freeze the zombie in place.

Shay's fingers followed along in the same dance, the same nimble spellcast. But no energy moved from her hands like it did Jed's.

Shay dropped her shoulders, defeated. "It didn't work." She flexed her fingers.

"Try again."

"I'm too human." Her voice was thick with disappointment.

Jed touched her shoulder. "I won't think less of you," he joked, the corner of his lips tipping up.

Shay swung at him. "You shit." Her fist landed on his bicep, and she moved to smack him again.

"I think you can do it," Jed said as he sprung away from Shay's fist. "You just need more time."

"It's been a long time. It's been forever."

Jed's eyes went wide and he held a finger to his lips. "Shhh. The dead will hear and come."

Shay paused and looked around. It wasn't long before the shuffling of feet started getting closer. "Shit."

"Let's go." Jed grabbed Shay's arm and tugged her in his direction.

The old Shay would have been pissed for not being asked which direction to run in, but she'd spent enough time with Jed to know that he had a knack for finding a way out. He'd never led her wrong. They'd spent plenty of time on the run after meeting on the Earthen plane.

Jed and Shay ran through the forest in a roundabout path toward the burning caves.

"Should we go to the cemetery?" Shay asked. "To lose them?"

"We can't risk bringing a horde to Thrush." He ducked under a low branch then held it up for Shay. "If we go back to the burning caves, they'll just wander away. They won't get close. Meg's there. They won't go near her."

"Not like the fast ones did?" Shay asked.

"The fast ones didn't follow the rules of Hell." Jed slowed to check their surroundings. "These slow ones will just move on." He motioned for her to move faster.

Jed and Shay moved quickly through the forest. Once they found the road, they ran parallel to stay hidden. Soon the moans of the walking dead got further and further away. Jed and Shay slowed, only to hear voices not far away. They both came to a stop and listened.

Shay ducked near a fallen tree and focused in the distance. She pointed. Jed crouched near a thick tree trunk coated in lichen and followed her line of sight.

There were three men dressed in black with white collars. Deacons.

Shay tapped her ear. Jed shook his head. Neither could hear what the Deacons were discussing. The dragging footsteps of the dead were getting closer. Jed and Shay were stuck in the middle.

Shay's heart thumped in her chest as they waited. She didn't like the feeling of being trapped. She'd spend too much of her life stuck between safety and the bliss of freedom. She turned to see the decaying forms of the dead as they meandered toward them and estimated how much time they had. At the rate they crept and how easily they were distracted, Shay figured it was less than six minutes before they needed to move again. She focused on the meeting of the Deacons in the road. Hopefully the men in black would be done by then.

———

SKEELE

Tukka grabbed Klaus by his beard, jerked until the giant Hellion dropped to one knee then rammed an elbow into his chest. Before Tukka could finish the move, Klaus twisted and kicked out his leg, tripping Tukka. The vigor that the two Hellions fought with might have worried a passerby, but the line of new recruits were watching with rapt attention.

Skeele clapped his hands together, ending the sparring match between the two. "Alright," he said with one hand raised, "double up and spar until one of you drops."

Skeele headed toward where Chel watched in the shadows of the trees as Tukka and Klaus rallied the new

Hellions. They'd almost replaced every Hellion from Lucifer's time. They wouldn't tolerate defectors or any Demon who didn't support Meg's throne.

"Did you find something?" Skeele asked Chel.

"The portals are still down. I checked them all. Nothing but rubble."

"And Demore's pond?"

"It's still there and under guard. We could drain it, but the water would likely collect there again and refill."

Skeele was silent as he contemplated.

"We found something," Chel pulled a metal syringe from his pocket. "There was Angel blood in it."

"Used to inject the Deacon in the cemetery." Skeele touched the syringe.

"It was," Chel confirmed. "We found it in the depths of Demore's pond."

"Put it somewhere safe," Skeele said. "Out of sight." He met Chel's black eyes with the sound of running footsteps in the woods behind them. With a nod, both Hellions readied themselves. "The fast ones are all dead."

"They were," Chel gripped his blade and it glowed, ready for battle.

Skeele drew his blade and sidestepped until he was a few yards from Chel. The footsteps got closer as did the sound of heavy breathing. Whoever was advancing wasn't trying to stay quiet.

Blue shone through the dapple light of the canopy.

"Wait," Chel motioned to hold their position. "I recognize that hair."

Jed and Shay broke through, running and panting.

The Hellions secured their weapons and let their guests enter the training fields. The two stopped to catch their breath.

Jed bent over, hands on his knees. "Damn, I need to run more." He wiped perspiration off his brow. "Been a long time. Too long." He patted his stomach. "Getting comfortable is never a good thing."

Shay coughed. "I was kind of enjoying not running for my life on a daily basis."

"Why were you running?" Skeele asked as he sheathed his blade before crossing his arms and looking down at the human and Nephilim.

"We were training in the forest, past the cemetery and a horde came," Jed said.

"They don't move that fast," Chel said.

Jed held up his hand as he said, "As we were leaving, we found three Deacons in the road not far from here. We had to wait for them to leave. The dead caught up."

"Deacons?" Chel's brows rose in attention.

"Did you hear what the Deacons were saying?" Skeele asked, suddenly interested.

"No," Jed shook his head. "We can show you where they were."

Skeele nodded and motioned for Chel to follow. He had to see if the Deacons had left anything behind.

Of course, they hadn't left a single thing behind, not even a footprint. But the Hellions did a thorough job of surveying the area and tracking back to the crossroads.

"Did they have a vehicle?" Skeele asked Jed.

"Not that we saw." Jed did his best to help but he wasn't trained in tracking, only running and hiding.

"You have a spell or something that could help us gain some insight?" Tukka asked.

Jed thought for a moment before reaching into his pocket to pull out the ages old notebook he carried with him. "I might have something. Let me look."

Shay stood close, watching Skeele as he searched. Skeele caught her eye more than a handful of times before he finally walked over to her and asked, "What?"

"You seem different," Shay said. She was straightforward and honest.

"Nothing's changed." Skeele ran a hand over his head and horns as one runs their hands through their hair in frustration.

"Sure." Shay stepped closer to Jed.

"Why do you ask?" Skeele said.

"You seem tired or sick, and you've lost a lot of weight. You're the Commander of the Hellions." Shay lowered her voice. "Maybe you should see that healer, Teari."

"Not necessary." Skeele walked away from the human and continued on his searching until Jed cleared his throat.

"I found something." He motioned to Skeele and Tukka. "It's a spell that can rewind time but only for a few moments."

Jed's fingers tapped and twisted as he chanted the spell, motioning in the area of the road where they'd seen the Deacons.

Transparent leaves rolled across the road before the images of the three Deacons appeared. They were see-through and faded, like Clea's wavering image. Ghosts of the past. Skeele moved closer and watched their lips as they spoke.

"Dead Newcomers." He heard them say. "Her condition." He couldn't make out the full conversation just bits of it. "Unlawful." Shit.

"What did they say?" Tukka asked.

Skeele pressed his lips together. His stomach felt like a boulder had dropped into it. Skeele had been haunted by the day he ate the Newcomer family. The Deacons found out. They were after him.

———

Meg

The long table in the dining room is overflowing with food. Roasted chicken, piles of grapes, chalices of wine. I pile my plate high but find that I can only pick at it. The days of gluttony on actual food seem to be gone. Or maybe I'm just moody.

Everyone came for Saturday night dinner. We've been trying to make it a weekly event now that things have calmed down. With the truce from the Seven Kingdoms of Heaven, things have been a lot more relaxed.

Nightingale and Shay are mashing sweet potatoes for Thrush to try after he gets done chomping on the corn cob in his hand.

"He has two teeth coming through," Noah says with a proud smile. He tugs two wings off the roast chicken and wags them at Thrush. "Watch this." Noah tosses the wings toward the roiling shadows on the ceiling then holds his palms open with a surprised look when they don't fall back down. "Surprise!"

Thrush looks up then back at Noah before giggling uncontrollably. The sound of his little voice brings a smile to everyone's face.

"Teeth already?" I ask. "Are they sharp?" I point to my own teeth.

"They aren't too sharp," Nightingale says as she combs Thrush's hair to the side. "Did you invite Gabriel and Teari to dinner?"

I nod. "A few times. But they're busy rebuilding." I use air quotes when I say rebuilding because I'm tired of them using it as an excuse.

Nightingale frowns as Thrush whacks her with the corn cob. "I'll give them some nightmares. Maybe that will make them reconsider blowing us off."

"Perfect." I chew on a piece of the roasted chicken.

Two bones fall from the ceiling as the baby Basilisk drop them.

"You'll spoil them," I warn Noah. "They'll be like begging dogs soon."

"Are there dogs down here?" Shay asks.

"All creatures," Noah says.

"Can we get a dog?" Jed asks. "Are dogs allowed?"

"You can get whatever you want," I say.

The door to the dining room opens. Skeele, Tukka, Chel, and Klaus enter.

"Hey, where ya been?" Noah asks.

The Hellions make their way to the empty seats. Shay looks uncomfortable. She gets that way when a group of Hellions are around. I remember when I felt like that. I watch her until she focuses on me. I smile and nod, hoping the gesture offers her some comfort and hoping it doesn't make me look like some weirdo who stares at people.

"We were tracking something," Skeele says. He glances at the empty seat next to me but sits next to Tukka on the other side of the table. I try not to take it personally. My stomach growls loudly.

"You want more?" Noah asks, pointing to a second roasted chicken. "There's ribeye too." He raises a platter piled with steaks.

I shake my head, but Skeele raises his hand and reaches for the steaks. "Hope the kitchen didn't overcook these."

"They undercook everything these days just to get out of the kitchen quicker," Noah chuckles. "They're too afraid of Meg showing up and emptying the fridge."

Skeele's brows raise in question.

"Shut up," I threaten Noah.

Skeele motions to me and mouths, "Are you hungry?"

He's asking if I need blood. I don't want to answer. "I'll have a steak." I stand and reach forward with my fork, jabbing a large steak and dropping it on my plate. They're rare, red juice seeping across my plate. My mouth waters. I dig in and eat the entire thing in record time.

Everyone talks and plans and reminisces. It's like a family dinner from a Lifetime Christmas movie. It makes me feel good. Even better is no one brings up the fact that Skeele fell down the stairs nearly drained of life a few weeks ago.

I remind myself that Thrush isn't a Nightjar, and Nightingale is back, and Teari has her hands again. Things are looking up. My stomach churns. I think I ate too fast.

"I'll be right back," I say as I stand and walk out of the dining room. I hate missing any time from these get togethers. I've waited all my life to have something like this. Even though I feel like an outsider. I feel like I can't relax, I can't let loose like I used to. It's probably the giant secret I've been keeping. It's eating me away from the inside. I've kept worse secrets. There's plenty I've done in the past that I didn't tell a soul about.

Just as I'm reaching for the dining room door, it opens. One of the new recruit Hellions is letting himself in and he has a visitor.

It's a Deacon.

"What the hell are you doing here?" I ask. I look to the Hellion, Shule, "Why is that thing in here? Why did you bring a Deacon to dinner?" Anger is welling up inside me. I don't want to see a Deacon. I don't want a Deacon to see our Saturday night dinner. It feels like a violation, and I hate it. Anger swells, my fingertips tingle. "Get him out of here!" I shout. "Deacons are not welcome here. Ever!"

My stomach is growls loud.

"Meg?" Skeele's voice sounds like it's a million miles away.

My mouth waters. Someone touches my arm. I turn and find Skeele standing there, looking concerned.

"What?" I ask.

"It's okay," he says. "Shule didn't know."

"It's not okay." Damn him for talking down to me. Damn him for interrupting.

"Get the Deacon out of here," Klaus says, making his way toward us.

"That's what I said." I look between the two Hellions. Am I dreaming? Am I in the Twilight Zone?

"Listen to me when I speak." I glare at Shule, and his face is stone. "Get the fucking Deacon out of here."

"We need to discuss your situation." The Deacon has the nerve to speak to me.

"Close your meddling lips." I warn. "How dare you come into my home, uninvited?"

"We've been trying to reach you," the Deacon says, his voice flat and even. He's not scared, not even a little. "We need to talk." His eyes focus on my stomach. "We need to talk about your *situation*."

"Don't," I warn. "Do not say one more word."

Suddenly, Klaus and Skeele are pushing me toward the hall and out the door.

"Get the fuck off me." I step away from them. "Get your hands off me and get this trash out of my home." I reach for my blade but remember I left it in my bedroom. I was trying to turn a new leaf, attending dinner without a weapon.

"Your situation needs–" the Deacon starts to say.

"No!" I turn my anger on Shule. "Why did you bring him in here?"

Shule lets out an awkward laugh, cocky. Arrogant. He opens his mouth to speak. But it's too late. The welled-up anger has to go somewhere, my body feels hot, thirst strikes. I can't listen to one more word. How dare they? Shule's jaw twitches. I move like a viper, teeth bared.

———

"Come with me," Skeele says quietly. I stand my ground and glare. "I don't want to force you." His voice is quiet so the others can't hear. How dare he?

I look down. There's blood on the floor. The Deacon is ghost pale. Shule is a mound of Hellion uniform.

Klaus looks uneasy.

Noah whispers to Nightingale and they disappear with baby Thrush.

Skeele says something but I can't hear him with the buzzing in my ears.

Jed grabs Shay and his fingers dance in spellcasting. They're gone before my next breath.

Shit. Our night is ruined. Goddamned Deacons and new recruits.

The Deacon backs up into the wide hallway. Skeele says something to Klaus in Hellspeak. Klaus moves around me and takes control of the Deacon situation.

"Let's go." Klaus motions to the Deacon. "Walk, Deacon. You know where the door is."

Saturday dinner devolves into me glaring at the black dress shirt of the Deacon as he walks away, watching his lips, making sure he mentions nothing about *my situation* to Klaus.

Skeele clears his throat.

I spin on my heel to face him. "What the hell was that?" I pace and find myself in the dining room with Skeele closing the door.

"What was what?" Skeele asks, crossing the room, giving me space.

I point, mad as a hornet. "You both interrupting me." I tug at my shirt, suddenly feeling claustrophobic. I can't breathe. "I had control of the situation. I don't need two Hellions butting in."

Skeele nods, his lips pressed into a straight line.

"What?" I shout.

Dark eyes land on me. "You didn't have control. You were very out of control."

"I was fine!"

Skeele spreads an arm toward the dining table loaded with uneaten food. "Then where did your guests go?"

A shudder of embarrassment rolls through me. "Home. I guess they were full."

Skeele chuckles. "That's not why."

"What do you even know? You know nothing." I point at the floor. "This is my realm. My castle. Mine."

"You live here alone?" He's very still.

I take one step forward, ready to pounce.

"You live here alone?" he repeats. "No one else lives under this roof? No one else eats at this table?" He rubs a finger across the polished dining table.

"How dare you?"

"How dare I question you?" he pushes.

The last spec of control leaves my body. I launch myself across the dining room. I toss an errant dining chair on its side.

"You want to fight." Skeele tips his head and cracks his neck with a smile. "Come on."

I reach for my blade, remembering I left it in my room. Pissed it's not on me, I grab a steak knife off the table.

Skeele's brows rise in jest. He reaches to the side and picks up two spoons.

"Don't be an idiot," I seethe, advancing toward him.

"Too late." He knocks the spoons together.

"It's your funeral." My stomach growls loudly. For a moment I revel in the hate of being controlled by blood. I pull a surge of energy from my toes and lurch forward, my knife slicing through the air in a swift arc.

Stainless steel clashes as Skeele crosses his spoons and catches the hilt of the steak knife. Serrated edge zips across spoon handles. In a powerful movement he thrusts the spoons forward and knocks my knife away. He dashes to the left, kicks a chair in my direction, and keeps going around the table.

I growl like an animal. "Running away?"

"Never." Skeele flashes a smile. "Just getting warmed up." He grabs a handful of grapes off the table and throws them at me.

I run toward him, step on the fallen chair, and leap onto the table. I kick a roasted chicken in his direction like a football. He leaps to the side, the carcass missing him and making a splat sound as it hits the wall. Grease leaves a giant mess on the wall as the chicken slides to its ultimate resting place.

"You know there are children starving in China?" Skeele picks up a fork and holds it out, threatening. "Probably some other places too."

"Then bring them these leftovers." I pick up a heavy candlestick and jump down, slipping on crushed grapes. "You gonna comb your hair with that?"

Skeele scrapes the tines across his bald head. "Feels good." He itches behind his ear and against his horns. "You want to touch them?"

"I'll rip them off your head," I promise. I drop the candlestick, pick up one of the fallen chairs, lift it over my head, and throw it at him.

Skeele moves to deflect the chair, but it barely makes it to him. The thing is heavy; it only goes a few feet in the air before falling on the ground with a loud thud and skidding across the floor.

"You're weak." Skeele kicks the chair against the wall. "Maybe you should eat something." He motions to a steak. "Or..." He grabs a knife off the table and holds it to his neck.

"Don't," I warn.

"Why not? It's what you want. It's what you need." He slices skin and a tiny drop of blood leaks from the cut.

"I'm fine." It takes every ounce of control to keep my body still and not jump on him. "Bastard."

"No. I'm not." He cuts his neck again. Two drops of blood trickle down his neck. He flicks his fingers. "Come on. We're fighting, remember?" His eyes crinkle. "Don't hold back."

I consider picking up the steak knife I dropped and throwing it at him, but I don't want any more blood. I'm not sure if I can control myself. My mouth waters, my stomach churns.

"It's been a long time since you invited me to your

room." He flicks a wrist. "A long time since you had fresh blood. And we both know what happens when you do this."

"I'm fine."

"Really?" he chuckles, the sound of his voice deep and warm. "This is not fine." He motions to my whole being. "You lost your shit on a Deacon. At dinner. You yelled at that poor young Hellion and killed him."

The drops of blood trickle down his neck and pool in the valley of his collarbone. I lick my lips.

Pounding on the dining room door echoes throughout the room.

"Go away," Skeele shouts.

"Is everything okay in there?" Tukka's voice shouts.

Skeele shoots me a questioning glance. "Are you okay?"

The drops of blood flow to the base of his neck and collect in a tiny pool.

"Perfectly fine."

"It's wonderful in here," Skeele shouts. "Like a vacation on the beach."

"I heard noise," Tukka says, trying the latch.

"Go away!" Skeele shouts looking toward the door.

That's my moment, his eyes are finally off me. I pitch toward him, ready to slam him to the ground. But my foot slips on a greasy piece of chicken and I lose my footing.

Skeele hurdles forward to catch me.

Chivalry should have been dead in this room. It might've saved him from me. I grab Skeele's arm at the elbow and twist, knocking him to the ground with me.

Skeele grunts. "You've been training with Tukka again?"

I shift my weight and wrap a leg around his middle. "Nope. Been watching Escape from New York."

Skeele rolls, taking me with him. His hand slides on a

pile of mashed potatoes that made it to the floor, probably when I kicked that chicken across the dining room table.

"Ugh," he groans. He reaches over and wipes his hand on my jeans.

"I'm not your personal napkin." I roll forward and shift my legs. I grab his sleeves and twist, locking his arms against his body.

"You got that move from old movies." Skeele lifts his legs, his thighs hitting me in the back and knocking me forward. I lose my balance and pitch forward, my nose inches from the pool of blood at his neck.

"Do it, Meg. You know you want to. Lick it off me."

"I'm full."

Skeele slams his feet on the floor and pushes up with his hips, tossing me off him as he rolls. Suddenly I am on my back, looking up at him.

"No." I thrash and slap. "No; this is not how it's going to end."

"Nothing has to end," he laughs, collecting my wrists and pressing my arms against my stomach. "We can keep going." He grips my wrists with his large hand, reaches for the knife that fell not far from us.

"Don't," I warn.

"What will you do, Meg?" He puts the hilt of the knife in his mouth, holding it as he slices his wrist. He spits the knife to the side. "Do it. I like it." His voice is low, promising, sinful. "Fuck me while you do it." He presses his bloody wrist against my lips.

"I hate you."

"I know." For a moment, the playfulness in his voice is gone, his expression turns pained. "Eat."

I drink his blood. He releases my wrists, and my hands move to his chest. His free hand roams my body, kneading and stroking. I grip his shirt and pull him closer, the heat between my thighs becoming unbearable. I lick the wound on his wrist and tug him closer. Firm lips dust mine for a moment before he bares his thick neck, pulsing veins, and small drops of blood from where he cut himself. I bite, I drink. Our hands are free to grab and touch. His blood is magic on my tongue, filling the void I've tried to ignore for so long. My brain buzzes with the *rush-rush-rush* of his heart pumping. Sweet and tingly like champagne, I drink like he's a never-ending fountain.

We roll until I'm on top. I tear at his shirt and feed from other places: the firm pectoral, the soft skin of his inner arm, the vee of his lower abdomen. He moans with each bite, his hips thrusting up in need. But I'm not ready for that yet. I'm too hungry. I waited too long. The bloodlust is strong, but my appetite is stronger. His hands are in my hair, gripping my scalp, tugging at my hair; the ache feels so good.

I climb his body like a siren slithering out of the ocean with one thing on my mind: fill this ache, fill this stomach, satisfy the need growing between my thighs.

Skeele rips my jeans apart and touches the warmth between my legs. "Christ," he whispers. "Why did you wait so long?"

I don't reply. I'm too busy licking his abdominal muscles before tasting. By the time I reach his neck, there isn't a spec of his body I haven't tasted, not a vessel I haven't fed from.

I'm ready to sate the bloodlust, brushing my lips against his, I settle his length at the softness of my center. We slide together. I moan.

Skeele is eerily silent. I stop my body. Stop taking what I want. Something more compels me to pause.

"Hey," I touch his face. "Hey."

Skeele's eyes are closed, his jaw slack, his head tipped to the side.

Oh no. I've done it again. Skeele is barely breathing. His pulse is faint. His breathing too slow. I shake his shoulder harder and harder, but he doesn't wake. I slap his cheek.

Panic rips through me. What if it was Thrush? What if it was Jed or Shay or Gabriel or Teari? A sickening feeling overtakes me. I am a danger to my friends. I am a danger to everyone. I can't be around them.

Poof. I go to my room. I don't bother to shower because I can do that where I'm going. I run to my closet and find my bag. I shove some clean clothes in there. I get dressed: jeans, a T-shirt and sturdy hiking sneakers. I take the time to brush my teeth and run my fingers through my hair.

I have one last thing before I go.

"I release you, Noah." I murmur into the darkness.

The thread that tethered us breaks. He is free. No more serving Meg. Noah can go be with his family. Something he never got to experience when he was alive on the Earthen plane because like the song goes, only the good die young.

Poof. I collect Skeele's body from the dining room. *Poof.* I tuck him into my bed because I actually do give a fuck. I can't leave him naked and drained on the dining room floor.

"I'm sorry," I whisper to Skeele. I steal a kiss and press my forehead against his. For a Hellion he's not so bad. Better than I ever expected. I shouldn't have been so harsh with him. I should have controlled my words when I was hungry and angry. But then, lust and hate are brethren, and I was speaking out of fear when I said some of those things. Still, he deserves better than what I have to offer. I told myself I was going to do better but I never did. Same old Meg. Same old mistakes. Not anymore.

———

Skeele

Skeele woke alone in the dark. His mouth was dry, his body ached. His head throbbed like someone had hit him with a mallet. He sat up too fast and was so dizzy he had to lay back again. He rubbed his eyes and sniffed the air. He was in Meg's room. He groaned, remembering all they'd done, the feel of her naked body on his. Her mouth, her...

He sat up again. "Meg?"

There was no one else. Something was strange, off. He got up and searched the room, the closet, and the bathroom. She wasn't there.

Skeele adjusted his clothing before going downstairs to the Hellion lair. He hadn't been taking her blood so he could no longer travel at will. He had to use his feet and he was starting to understand why Meg just chose to *poof* from place to place half the time.

The lair was empty except for Chel looming in the shadows like always.

"Hey," Skeele said as he went to the fridge and took out four bags of blood.

"Hungry?" Chel asked.

Skeele chuckled to himself. "Yeah."

"Where have you been?" Chel asked, sounding annoyed.

"I've been here."

"We haven't seen you for two days. And no one has seen Meg."

Skeele paused after swallowing a mouthful of blood. "Two days?"

He rubbed his face. "Did you look for me?"

Chel raised his hands, in defeat, annoyed. "Everywhere."

"Meg's room?" Skeele asked.

"No one answered the door."

"Why didn't you go in?"

Chel made a face. "And have her bite our heads off? No thanks. After the other night, everyone was too afraid of her. Even Noah."

Skeele drank from another bag and collected his thoughts.

"Goddamnit." He slammed his fist down on the bar top and ran out of the room.

Skeele ran up the stairs, four steps at a time, then he ran down the hall and burst through Meg's door. He turned on all the lights. He checked her closet. There was a bag missing and a pair of sneakers. He checked the shelf where she stored her blade. It was still there but covered with a leather sheet.

Her clothes were haphazardly spilled on the floor and dug through. Wherever she was going, she left in a hurry.

"No, Meg." Skeele gripped his horns and held in a roar of defeat.

Meg was gone.

Warm nights, Dark beaches

Florida seems like a good choice. The panhandle this time. I'm ready for white, sandy beaches and turquoise water. Anything closer to Miami brings back memories of Reuben. I shiver. I don't want to remember Reuben and his dark void of a head as the Scarecrow.

The first thing I do is head to the bank. There's a branch down here. I walk inside and show the teller my license.

"You're going to want to get a new one of those." She taps the card as she slides it back to me. "You look different."

"I do?" I bend down to get a glimpse of my reflection in the glass separating us. I look at the picture on my license. "I guess I do," I agree. "I'll go to the DMV tomorrow."

"How can I help you today?" The teller is young, blonde, and cute like she just graduated from high school and wakes up every day with an ass-load of energy to count money and smile at the people of Perdido Key.

"I need to check my balance and I need some cash." I

make a few calculations and then round up. "Five-thousand cash."

The girl taps on her computer keys. "No problem."

A man in a suit walks up behind her and they whisper to each other. My stomach sinks. Shit. I turn to look at the door and the video cameras in the corners of the lobby. I'm the only one here. My heart thumps.

The scratchy beeps of the printer pull me out of my panic.

"Okay, I just need you to sign here." The teller slides me a slip of paper. She rests the tip of her pen on the numbers in the corner. "This is your balance."

I lean forward and see a lot of zeroes. Thankfully the money I inherited has just been sitting in savings collecting interest.

"Just a heads-up," she says as I sign, "anything over ten thousand will require a forty-eight hour notice to pull."

"Gotcha." I set the pen down when I'm done signing. She slides me an envelope of money. I tuck it in my bag.

"Do you want to count that?" she asks. "Once you leave–"

"I trust you," I interrupt her, eager to get the heck out of the bank.

"Have a good day." She smiles and goes back to tapping on her computer keyboard.

I step into the hot Florida sun and start walking down the street. I smile to myself. The Deacons will never find me here. They're better off trekking me down to sell me an extended car warranty than knocking on my door to discuss my condition. Fuck my condition.

———

"I need a room. Facing the beach." I tap my fingers on the countertop and search the lobby for a gift shop. I need sunglasses in a bad way. My head is starting to throb from the sunlight. It's worse than Heaven. I don't remember the Earthen plane to have such a punishing sun.

"I'll need an ID and credit card." The man behind the desk stares at me.

"I have an ID." I slide it over to him then I search my wallet for an old credit card. It's my lucky day, this sucker doesn't expire for three months.

"You're going to need a new one of these soon." He waves the ID.

"I know. I look different."

"No," he says. "This expires at the end of the year."

"It does?" I take the ID back. "Well, I'll be damned."

"The DMV here is pretty quick. If you're moving here, you'll need residency." His brows rise. "Or are you just visiting? Nearly half the check-ins have been transplants from New York. Uh, the room is four hundred a night."

"Ew." I make a face and look at his name tag. It says Alex. "I used to live here so that makes me better than any typical transplant. I'll take the room for the week. Until I find a realtor."

"Oh yeah?" Alex asks as he scans keycards with his machine. "Where?"

"Near Miami."

Alex smiles and hands me the hotel room cards. "This is a lot quieter than Miami." He winks and I wonder if it's because he's friendly or a serial killer. I should probably work on my trust issues.

———

My next stop is getting a car. I can't be walking everywhere in this heat, and I need to find a house to hole up in. I'd rather be spending the day at the beach but instead I'm sitting in a chair at Crystal Automotive waiting for the sales attendant to confer with his manager about the drop-top Mustang I'd like to buy.

The two men walk toward me, and I stand. I force a smile, trying my best to remember my manners since I haven't been on the Earthen plane in a while.

"We have to disclose to you that the vehicle you want was manufactured before the Zombie War."

"Okay." Jeeze, I didn't realize... I need to read some newspapers and get a clue. The last time I was here the Earthen plane was a shit mess. But the little town of Perdido Key seems to have put itself back together pretty well. There's no blood splatter or brain chunks or rotting bodies, that I've seen.

"It just might... smell a little strange if you leave it in the sun with the windows closed for a long period of time. We've thoroughly cleaned it." One of the men looks at the papers he's holding.

It might smell. Great. The smell of coffee made me spew chunks one morning, I'm sure the smell of death might do the same.

"What else have you got?" I ask. "Money isn't an issue."

The two men look at each other and then walk me toward a sparkling new Jeep Grand Cherokee.

"Perfect. Let's sign papers," I say.

———

It takes me four days to drive to all of the Catholic churches near Perdido Key. Holy Spirit Catholic Church on Gulf Beach Highway is the first to lose its holy water supply and any fountains on the premises. St. Thomas by the Sea is next. Then Saint John the Evangelist church. Then Little Flower Catholic Church. Finally, Our Lady Queen of Martyrs.

The fountains could be portals and destroying the holy water was just something extra because water is a conduit and I'm sure holy water could let lots through. I have to destroy it all, just to be safe. I smashed them.

When I return to the hotel from my last night of destruction, I extend my stay by another week.

"Having trouble finding a home?" Alex asks.

"Yes," I lie.

Alex opens a drawer and digs around for a moment. "Here." He hands me a card. "Check with Stacy. She's my aunt."

"Hey, thanks, Alex." I tuck the card in my pocket. "I'm going to call her in the morning."

What a great guy Alex is. So helpful. He has no idea what I am and what I've done. I like to keep the bar low. It's the best way to start a relationship.

As I walk to my room, my stomach grumbles loudly. Shit.

———

I dream of volcanoes in the ocean. Hot lava bubbling and splashing on rooftops setting everything near the coast on fire. There are coyotes running through my backyard. I'm watching it all and talking to a bird with brown wings and a white chest and telling it there's no volcanoes in Florida. Perdido Key is safe.

"Perdido Key?" the bird asks. "Are you at a roach hotel or something nicer?"

"I'm staying at Johnny's On the Beach."

The bird flutters off.

I wake up grumpy and hungry. The scar on my arm aches. There are a dozen donuts from yesterday on the dresser in a half open box. I rub my eyes and wish for fresh coffee. Noah isn't here so I have to be a big girl and drag my ass out of bed to go find some.

I put on the clothes I wore yesterday. They smell damp, like rain. I need to get more clothes and find a laundromat. My standards are pretty low but dirty, wet clothes is where I draw the line. I brush my teeth and wash my face then head out.

Alex isn't at the desk. It's an older man with a gray beard and waxed mustache twisted into points. I wave and try to act normal; not like the ruler of Hell in hiding. Not like a vampire looking for blood. I think it works since he waves back and wishes me a good morning.

I head to my car, drive to a McDonald's drive through, and order enough food for three people. I eat it all in the parking lot of a Marshall's department store. When I'm done pigging out, I'm going to one stop shop.

I buy shorts, tanks, clean underwear, a few bikinis, flip-flops, deodorant, and body spray so I don't smell like rain-water for the entire day. I wander by the book section and a book with birds on it catches my eye. *Birds of the World* it reads. The book draws me like an omen. I flip through the pages and land on a page with a little brown bird. A

Nightingale. Something pings on my brain. I remember the dream I had last night. Shit. That wasn't just a random dream about apocalyptic volcanoes in Florida and cute little birds. Nightingale is back to invading my dreams.

I jog to the checkout and pay for everything. This has been the world's worst game of hide-and-seek. I gave up my location in record time. As I'm handing over my bank card, I tell myself that there are no portals in Hell. We destroyed them all. There's no way for anyone to get out and find me.

There are no portals in Hell. There are no portals in Hell. There are no portals in Hell.

"What's that, dear?" the cashier asks, her saggy upper arms waggling as she hands me back my credit card.

"Nothing," I reply as I grab my bags and run to my Jeep.

I'm going to have to find a new place to stay. I dig through my wallet until I find the realtor card Alex gave me. Stacie Realty on Gongora Drive. It's on the other side of the island.

I put the pedal to the metal and drive there as fast as I can. On the way, I open my windows and spray myself with the body spray I got from Marshalls, hoping I don't just wind up smelling like rainwater and cheap perfume.

I follow Perdido Key Drive until the turn for Gongora comes into view. The realtor office is a small house with giant elephant ear plants growing near the front porch. After parking, I walk to the door, feeling like I need a hot shower. I should've cleaned myself up before I came here. I shake my clothes, hoping to get rid of the smell of too much body spray.

The sign on the door says to let myself in, so I do. There's a lady with dangling flamingo earrings.

"Can I help you?" she asks, with a mild southern accent.

"I'm looking to buy a home," I say.

"Okie dokie." The sign on the desk says Stacy and I wonder if it's a typo. She rolls in her chair to pick up a stack of papers, then rolls back. "Have a seat. Have you been pre-approved for a loan, dear?"

"I have cash."

"Do you have proof of funds?"

I dig in my bag for the receipt from the bank the other day. "It's in here somewhere."

"While you're looking, tell me what kind of house you want. A condo, a single-family, new construction town-house?" She talks with her hands moving.

"Something close to the beach and... not too fancy." I find the receipt and show it to her.

Stacy flattens the strip of paper on her desk and makes a surprised face. "Well, with this you can get whatever your little heart desires." She slides the paper back. "But let me pull up what we have for sale. Come around here." She pats on a free chair that's behind her desk.

I sit and smell myself. I tell myself I don't care. I used to smell worse. There were weeks I didn't bathe when I was a kid. "Sorry, I got stuck in the rain, my jeans are damp."

She flicks her wrist. "We get all types in here." She doesn't even wrinkle her nose as she points to the computer screen. "Okay these are what's on the market now. This one is near the beach. She points at a little bungalow with a rusty green roof and surrounded by palm trees.

"I like that one."

"You don't want to see more?" She turns to face me.

"I'm just looking for a home. Something simple."

"Well, eager beaver. Let me call over there and see if we can go look at it."

I lean back in my chair as she makes the phone call. *Woosh-woosh-woosh*. The pulsing in her neck draws my attention. Saliva pools in my mouth. It's been nearly a week since I almost killed Skeele. I get up and move near the door so I'm not tempted to do something illegal. Like suck every last drop of blood out of Stacy's body and leave her carcass for the next buyer to find.

Stacy hangs up the phone. "Let's go." She opens a drawer and gets out her purse before meeting me at the door. "Do you want me to drive you? Or do you want to follow me?"

"I'll drive myself."

I run to my Jeep and wait for her to pull out of the driveway. It's better if I drive myself, then I won't be tempted to lean over and bite her neck. I won't be tempted to grab the steering wheel and... I click the lock on my door. Focus, Meg. Focus.

———

The street is Parasol Place. There's a crumbling sound as I drive over the white, crushed shell driveway. The house is small and painted peach, with green shutters and white picket fencing across the tiny front yard. Two red Adirondack chairs are on the front porch.

Stacy waves me to the front door. She's messing with a box hanging from the handle.

"I really like this," I say as I get closer.

She gets a key out of the box and enters the house. I follow. The interior is dated but everything that matters works. There's water, a shower, a kitchen, and appliances.

"I'll take it. But, can I get the furniture and curtains?" I ask.

"I can ask the sellers." Stacy texts on her cell phone.

"How fast can we close?" I ask.

"Money talks."

"Tonight?" I ask. "I'll pay fifty thousand over asking price. And I want the furniture."

Sleeping in a stranger's bed seems weird. But I slept on a mattress on the floor for fifteen years, and I'm pretty certain it was pulled from a dumpster. At least this place smells clean and I can wash the sheets or buy new linens another day.

———

Stacy from Stacie Realty makes the magic happen. I wire the money and have a key in my hand by seven p.m. She meets me at the hotel for the final paperwork.

As I'm leaving, bags in hand, I notice Alex is working the desk.

"Hey, Stacy!" He waves.

I say my goodbyes and thank-yous and amaze myself with my good manners. Gabriel would be proud. Teari too. The Hellions would be flabbergasted.

I drive to Marshall's, buying a new coffee maker and a few mugs, then head to the little house on Parasol Place.

I like the sound of the Jeep's tires crunching on the seashell drive. It doesn't feel like home, but I've spent most of my life with nothing feeling like home. I think of my little white house in Gouverneur. It was the first home I had to myself. But then Jim came along, and home became something I'd rather not remember.

I unlock the door to my little beach house, go inside, and take a breath of relief. If I never leave the house, no one from Hell will find me. They won't be searching every home in Perdido Key, and I didn't leave a forwarding address at the hotel.

I get my packages out of the Jeep and the first thing I unpack is a fancy coffee maker and two bags of coffee. I wash the mug and leave it to dry by the blue, ceramic sink.

If I do anything during this time on the Earthen plane, it will be to never sleep again. I'm not even going to blink, I can't risk giving up my hiding place to Nightingale.

———

SKEELE

Skeele stood in the living room of the chapel in the cemetery. Scowling, with arms crossed, he waited for Nightingale to exit the bedroom where she was putting down Thrush for a nap.

"Can't you go do it?" Skeele asked Noah.

"Baby wants his momma. And baby gets what baby wants." Noah sat down and crossed his legs. "Want something to eat while you wait?"

"No." There was one thing that Skeele wanted and that was to know exactly where Meg was. He'd come the instant Noah had news only to find out it wasn't Noah, but Nightingale who'd tracked her down.

The door to the bedroom finally opened and Nightingale skated through. She turned to close the door softly and held her finger to her lips when she faced the impatient Hellion.

She whistled a light trill and waggled her fingers at Noah. He smiled. The entire scene tore at Skeele's heart. He'd never have something like this, a family, a child. Or someone who loved him unconditionally and wasn't afraid to show it.

Skeele closed his eyes and took a deep breath. He reminded himself that he was eager to let her use him. He told Meg himself, *use me*. He'd said it too many times. And that's exactly what she did. He got what he asked for. She warned him not to get attached, so he didn't. At least that's what he let her believe.

"I know you've been waiting," Nightingale said as she skated closer to him. "Meg is safe. I could hear the ocean and cars."

"What ocean?" Skeele asked, wanting more details.

Nightingale held up a hand to slow him down. "She's on the Earthen plane. Last time she ran away there she was in Florida. She told me some things before she woke up. I'm sure she's realized it was me visiting her dreams by now. She's in Perdido Key. She's safe." Nightingale leans closer to Skeele. "But she's hungry. Very hungry. This will not end well." Nightingale gave him a knowing look. "There's lots of human blood there. Fresh blood. And they don't stand a chance against the ruler of Hell." Nightingale cleared her throat. "The Earthen plane doesn't have many people left after the Zombie War. If she loses control, she's at God's mercy. That is his plane."

Skeele moved to the door as though crossing realms was nothing more than a hop across a puddle. "I'll go get her."

"Slow down, homeboy." Noah closed the door. "You can't just ram it on in there and drag her back here by her hair."

"She won't do what others tell her," Nightingale said.

"You're going to have to trick her." Noah looked Skeele up and down. "You're going to have to glamour yourself. Change your name. Fit in with the humans."

"Fine," Skeele said. "I can do that."

"You need to do it really good," Noah said. "She'll run somewhere else." There was a knock on the door. Noah opened it and let Jed inside. He was carrying a small pouch.

"One last thing," Noah said. "You're going to need a few tattoos, so the Angels don't come looking for you and try to throw you out. A Hellion being on the Earthen plane is not a light event. Sparrow killed and destroyed. The grouping before found Meg and..." Noah pressed his fingers to the bridge of his nose and took a deep breath. "They can't find you. She can't know it's you. The Earthen plane is her safe place. She always runs there. She always runs home."

"This is her home," Skeele corrected.

Noah smiled, but it was a little bit sad. "It is and she's almost accepting of that."

Jed sat at the table near the window and opened his bag. He took out pots of black ink and his tattoo gun. "Maybe you can change that," Jed suggested.

Noah herded Skeele to sit across from Jed and motioned for him to pull up his sleeves.

"So, what's your style?" Jed asked. "Eagles, Celtic crosses, Chinese characters?" His brows rose in question. "Please don't tell me it's tribal art."

S keele was at the chapel for hours and when he left, he'd gained a textbook worth of knowledge about the Earthen plane and how to pretend to be human. They'd even given him some dating advice. The night air felt strange against the forest images tattooed from his wrists to his elbows. It was Vermont. And underneath the coniferous trees were deep runes that would hide him from the Angels and other otherworldly creatures.

Skeele took to Hellsky and flew back to the burning caves as fast as he could. He had bags to pack and needed to have a conversation with the other Hellion Commanders. He wasn't sure how long he'd be gone.

―――

MEG

I binge on movies to pass the time. I order takeout and drive to McDonald's on the other side of the bridge to get coffee twice a day. I tell myself that if someone from Heaven or Hell is here, they are less likely to notice me through the tinted windows of my Jeep so it's a safe option. But I smashed all those fountains at the surrounding churches. If someone were coming for me, it's going to take a while.

Today, the beach is loud. There's maybe twenty other people here but all I can hear are their heartbeats pumping through their bodies. The worst of it are the kids. Their little hearts pump super fast. With the *hush-hush-hush* of it all, I can't focus on anything. I pack up my chair and towel and walk back to the house.

I won't drain anyone's blood. I won't drain anyone's blood. I won't drain anyone's blood.

I get in my Jeep and go for more coffee. My first stop is the Publix grocery store across the Theo Baars Bridge. Thunderheads billow in the distance, lightning starts over the ocean. I challenge myself to get in and out of the store before it rains.

People are staring at me. I lick my lips. This is danger-ous. I keep my sunglasses on, pull my hat low, and nearly run with my cart to the coffee aisle. I grab five bags of coffee then head to the refrigerator section for creamer. I pass the fresh meat in coolers and pause. I have an idea. I grab the bloodiest steaks and roasts I can find. If I can't have human blood, maybe some ultra-rare steaks will do.

As I'm leaving the grocery store. The storm thickens and starts rolling in from the Gulf. Right on time. Thunder booms. I run to my car and just as I close the door, the rain pours down. I drive back to the beach house, the bloody steaks calling my name. Just as I turn onto Parasol Place lightning strikes the lamp post.

"Ah!" I scream to myself and take my foot off the gas. My heart is beating a thousand times a minute and the hairs on my arms rise.

If I didn't know better, I'd say God was trying to scare me out of his realm. Maybe this isn't my safe haven. Even though Lucifer and the Archangels told me God was gone. There is some presence on the Earthen plane. God or not.

———

Skeele

Skeele carried a single leather bag and was dressed in jeans, a short sleeved button-down with palm trees printed on it, a baseball cap, and sneakers. He'd preferred his Hellion boots, but Jed and Shay told him they'd draw too much attention. The sneakers felt strange on his feet.

"Show me how to do the glamour again," Skeele asked Jed.

Jed told him what words to say. "It won't fade, not until you come back here," Jed said.

"Are you sure?" Skeele didn't want to be a sitting duck

on the Earthen plane. The runes would hide him but if he was walking around the Earthen plane looking like a Hellion, everyone was bound to notice.

Jed stood on the edge of the pond near Demore's cabin. It was night and the other Hellions were keeping the dead of Hell at a distance. They couldn't risk any falling into the portal and making it to the Earthen plane.

"You're going to do fine," Nightingale said with a chirp that sounded like a hiccup.

They were all wary of Skeele going alone. He hadn't spent much time on the Earthen plane and the bags of blood in his pack weren't going to last long. Time was not on his side. He had to woo Meg and get her back where she belonged. Since her disgust was clear and she wanted nothing to do with him on a relationship level, Skeele would have to pretend to be someone else, someone Meg might cling to in her darkest hours.

Jed did his thing. He chanted strange words and his fingers danced in rhythmic spellcasting. A small area of the pond bubbled and then opened up into a dark void. Shay stood by, soaking up the lesson in opening portals to other realms, her fingers tapping in copycat motions. Now that Thrush had his parents, Shay had nothing better to do than learn everything Jed offered.

Jed paused his chanting and nodded at Skeele. It was time for him to go. Skeele jumped through the portal and was transported to the Earthen Plane.

———

Skeele landed in a crouched position on the white sandy beach of Perdido Key. Sand slid under his feet. His back felt loose without his wings. The moonlight gave him some light to see by and he was thankful that no one else was on the beach to see him arrive. He stood and took in his surroundings. He had hours before sunrise, so he went straight to where Meg was supposed to be.

Skeele walked Perdido Key Drive until he saw the sign for Johnny's On the Beach. The hotel was small but the light out front flashed vacancy. Skeele tipped his hat lower and went inside.

The guy at the desk looked at the clock when Skeele walked through the door. "Just get into town?"

"Yeah," Skeele said. "I need a single room."

The guy at the desk tapped on his computer keys. "I need and I.D. and the room is two-fifty a night for a parking-lot view room."

Skeele pulled a roll of cash out of his pocket and a blank I.D. card Jed made with magic.

The guy took the cash and made a keycard. "Room two-twenty-five." He pointed toward a hall to the left.

Skeele walked the long hallway of the motel with slow footsteps. He'd never been to a place like this, and the smells were overwhelming to him. There was food, mold, liquor, dirt, body odor, sex. He wondered if this was how humans lived on the Earthen plane, like animals in the forest. The one thing he couldn't smell was Meg. Either she covered her scent here or she wasn't staying at this motel any longer.

Skeele stopped at room 225 and opened the door. The first thing he did was cover the large mirror over the dresser with a sheet. He wanted to break it because even with the glamour, his reflection was his true self. He stood in front of the sheet-covered mirror, tore the sheet down. He was a Hellion in the reflection, his horns tucked under the baseball hat and sharp teeth behind his lips. He punched the mirror and the glass shattered.

He stashed the blood from his bag in the mini fridge. He could survive on regular food for a while. But he might need the cold blood depending on how long he was on the Earthen plane.

In the morning, he left the room and searched the hotel for any sign of Meg. Skeele stood outside every room and took a deep breath. He grumbled when he concluded Meg was no longer at the hotel. He assumed she must've realized Nightingale had tracked her and got out of there. Skeele made his way to the lobby. He picked through the pamphlets for restaurants, beaches, state parks, and attractions. He took a few and tucked them in his pocket. Noah mentioned taking Meg on dates to new places. He'd have to start with the pamphlets because he didn't know jack about this place. If they were in Hell he'd take her to the black-sanded beaches and salt mines. But she'd told him not to get attached, so he planned nothing.

The sun pouring through the front doors of the motel lobby was bright and reminded him of the punishing sunlight of the Seven Kingdoms of Heaven. Skeele tipped his hat down to shade his eyes and exited the hotel intending to track Meg.

———

Skeele wandered the walkway along the beach and stopped at one of the little tourist shops where he picked out a pair of sunglasses. Further down Perdido Key Drive there were medical buildings and a pharmacy. He went back to the hotel intending to search that section of town in the morning.

Skeele stopped at the library on his way home. He didn't have a library card, but he could browse. He nodded at the woman sitting behind a desk.

"We close in thirty minutes," she said as he passed, snapping her gum.

"I won't be long," he assured her.

Skeele stopped at the magazines and thumbed through them. He had to get a quick education about the Earthen plane if he was going to trick Meg into thinking he was something other than a Hellion. And he needed a new name. After reading most of the front covers of the magazines, he decided Kal would do. It was close enough to his real name he would answer to it. Less chance for confusion.

———

MEG

I leave my house and drive down River Road toward the clinic. I made an appointment to end this. It's a very hush hush, unlabeled office. They do things that some might consider unethical, things that a decent human being might never do. Unfortunately, I'm not a decent human being any longer.

Saliva fills my throat, threatening vomit all over my new car. I grab a bag from the door pocket and hold it in my lap. The nausea this morning is horrific. It's like the creature in my belly knows it's eviction day. I'd be pissed too. I'm a shitty host. I doubt growing on coffee and shame is a delightful diet.

Giant white clouds are rolling over the ocean. They look

like a mountain and there's a layer of darker clouds below them. Just as I pull into the small parking lot, rain drops start hitting my windshield.

I check the clock. I've got five minutes. I'd like to run in and avoid the rain but the lady on the phone told me not to arrive early. She said arrive right on time due to the delicate matters they handle there. The cloudy day turns into a monsoon too quick.

I find a peppermint in the console and pop it in my mouth, hoping it will help with the nausea. I dig around for an umbrella but don't find one.

In typical Florida manner, the rainstorm comes with thunder and lightning. Lightning strikes near the beach and across the bridge to the mainland.

9:55 am. It's my time. I open the door to the Jeep and get out. Without an umbrella, I ready myself to run. I slam the door closed and hold a hand over my eyes. I leap over a puddle to get to the sidewalk. There's tall shrubbery hiding the front door. Just as I step up onto the porch, lighting strikes the roof. The hairs on my arms and neck stand up. I smell smoke. I look up to see fire starting near the corner of the building. Dark smoke turns to orange flame. The door opens and a handful of people run out.

"Do you have an appointment?" a dark-haired lady with giant red glasses asks me.

"Yeah."

"The building is on fire. You'll have to reschedule."

She leaves me standing alone in the rain, next to the burning building. Sirens blare in the distance. I turn around and walk back to my Jeep, no longer caring that I'm being doused with rain. I get in my vehicle and don't bother putting on my seatbelt. I start the car and drive away. I make my way to Perdido Key Drive and turn onto the unnamed road with a local pizza joint. A medium cheese and two-liter of cola. All for myself. I cry when I take the first bite of pizza. I tell myself it's because the crust is so chewy and the cheese so stringy and the sauce light and sweet, just like I like it. I've never had more delicious pizza. I've never hated life more than this moment. I had a plan and now it's fucked.

———

The next day, I call the number to the office that went up in flames yesterday. No one answers. I take it as a sign to come up with a new life plan. Leaving my little house I walk to the beach, the seashell driveway coating my flip-flops in white dust. After finding a quiet spot on the sand I sit on a towel, kick off my sandals, and dig my feet into the sand.

Since my standards are low and I'm alone on the beach, I take a raw steak out of my bag. I unwrap the one pound of bloody meat, rolling the plastic down to cover my fingers. Then I eat the entire thing like a starved man biting into the best bacon cheeseburger of his life. It's messy and I wipe my mouth on my arm more than once until there's red streaks left behind.

"Are you okay?" an old man with a white beard is staring at me.

I smile, then stop because my teeth are probably coated in cow blood. "I'm wonderful."

My stomach has stopped growling and I can no longer hear the *hush-hush-hush* of every passing person's heart within a mile radius of my location.

"You have the zombie disease?" the bearded man asks. "I thought they were all killed."

"No." I chew and swallow and wipe at my face.

He moves away from me. "You should really see a doctor then."

That's probably the best recommendation I've received in a long time.

———

I sit in a cold, bright waiting room.

"Meg," the girl at the desk calls and waves for me to go to her.

"I'm Meg."

"I need photo ID and insurance."

I get out my walled. "I'm paying cash." I slide her my ID.

She scans it, pausing before handing it back to me. "You're going to need a new one."

"I know it expires."

She stares.

"I look a little different too."

She blinks twice. "It says you live in New York."

"I used to."

"Half of New York is uninhabitable. I'd change my address."

"Sure." I thank her for the guidance.

There's an old man in the corner watching the news. After fifteen minutes they call me back to an equally cold and bright exam room.

A tired-looking man enters the room. "Good morning, Ms. Clark." The doctor uses a touch screen iPad. "So, you're having trouble staying awake?"

"Yes." I press my hands together and try not to act sketchy.

The doctor looks at my face. "You look tired."

"That's the problem. I'm always tired. I can't stay awake."

"Hm."

"I've tried coffee and energy drinks."

"Do they work?"

"Sometimes."

"Have you ever been diagnosed with narcolepsy?"

"What's that?" I ask.

"I'll take that as a no." The doctor taps on his computer screen. "Let's try a stimulant. The other option is antidepressants."

"I don't think I need antidepressants."

"Uh-huh. After the zombie apocalypse half the country is on them." He sighs. "They're on backorder anyway. If you find any let me know. What pharmacy do you want to use?"

"The one down the street."

He focuses on the computer for a few moments. "You should have some testing. Stop by the lab for some blood-work. You want an MRI?"

"For what?" I ask.

"To check out your brain. They're expensive and I see you are self-pay."

"I have money."

"It can cost up to three grand." His brows rise.

"Nah," I dismiss the idea with a wave. "I'd rather not." What if they find nothing in my skull, or worse, what if they find something?

"Okay. Do the lab work. Try the meds. Come back and see me in a week. Unless you have a primary doctor you usually see."

"I don't."

"Most don't." He stands and nods. "Thank you, have a nice day."

Wow. Times have changed. He didn't even listen to my heart or my lungs. What if I was a fucking robot sitting here? He'd never know. What if I had no heart, no pulse, no lungs? He just collected my two-hundred bucks and did a little clickety-clack on his computer and walked out the door.

I leave the urgent care and stop at the lab next door. Seems everything is electronic these days, no more slips of paper to carry around with doctor scribble. The nice young man at the lab takes five vials of blood. I think I should have skipped that, but I want this doc to help me out so I'm going to do what he orders. I probably shouldn't be giving up much of my blood since I have nothing to replace it with.

I drive to the pharmacy and pick up the pills. I twist the cap and pour out two into my palm. I swallow them down with a swig of cold coffee.

———

I sit on the beach and watch two college looking lads play volleyball. They're sweaty, their abs glistening and biceps flexing in the hot panhandle sun. I could bite every inch of them. I could lick them both from head to toe and leave them emptier than a cheerleader's head during final exams week. But that wouldn't be nice. Do better, Meg. Do better.

I press my lips together and focus on the magazine in my hands. I don't really care about the latest celebrity scandal but there's post-Zombie War info in this. It seems all the tabloids have taken to the post-War stories, interviews, and recollections. There are stories from famous actors who survived all locked up in their mansions with plenty of food and security. What a crock.

I stop flipping the pages to the magazine when a picture of a bunch of kids catches my eye. There's probably twenty of them, varying ages. The story is about all the children turned orphans after the Zombie War. I read the article. They're searching for families to adopt them. It must suck, losing everything in the Zombie War; your family, your parents, your home. I lost a lot in the Zombie War too. My boyfriend, my dignity, all the blood in my body–I glance down at my chest–a perfectly good tattoo. I should get that fixed.

The article gives me an idea. Since the clinic was destroyed and I haven't grown the balls to find another one further away, I consider the alternative. If I can't get rid of the creature growing in my belly, I can leave it behind for someone else to deal with. I don't feel as guilty. At least this decision won't end in death. The images from Teari's book flash through my mind. Mothers being torn apart by tiny monsters with little horns and sharp claws. Blood every-where and torn open vaginas and stomachs. She assured me that wouldn't happen. But I trust no one. If I survive the delivery, God can keep his monstrosity on the Earthen plane. No one needs to know. I glance at the runes on my arms. Maybe I'll lower my standards even more and tattoo the baby like we considered doing to Thrush. Maybe if no one knows and no one can find it, then I'm absolved of guilt and wrongdoing. Skeele won't ever have to know. I'll just tell Teari I miscarried and bled it out one night. She'll never have to know either.

I pack up my beach chair and go home to call the adop-tion agency listed in the article.

———

"Ms. Clark." The doctor sits down and rolls his stool closer to me. "We tried to call you about your labs."

"I don't have a cell phone or answering machine." I'm probably the only person on the Earthen plane without one. It makes me feel special.

"I see that. You should get one. Or a secretary to sit at your house and take calls." His dry tone really hits.

"Nah. I lean back in my chair. I like the freedom."

He smirks. "You won't be enjoying it for much longer."

"Huh?"

"You have elevated hCG."

"No clue what that means." I tap my fingers on my legs.

"You're pregnant."

My mouth goes dry. I sit up and choke back the bile rising in my throat. I know this already; I just don't want any more evidence of the truth.

"You didn't know?"

I shake my head. Lies.

"You have to stop taking the stimulants." He clicks on his computer. "You can't take them pregnant. Do you have an obstetrician in mind? You'll need to find one."

"Can't you do it?" My throat is dry, feels like I've been chewing on cotton.

"I can't." He focuses on me. "This is unexpected?"

I nod.

"Do you want to be pregnant? These are dark times, but we are rebuilding; we lost a lot of good people in the zombie war."

"I don't want it." Tears burn in the corners of my eyes. Saying the words out loud sounds horrible. I was scared but I'd wanted Elise. This thing inside me, it's not the same.

He makes a face of disappointment. "I'll write for the morning after pill. We caught this early. This is why you are so tired." He sets his computer down and leans forward. I notice his badge. Dr. Jordan. "Give it a week. If you're still sure, then take the pill. Either way, stop the stimulants until you've decided."

"Sure." I stand, ready to run the hell out of there and bury my head in the sand from humiliation.

"I'll send over a prescription for prenatal vitamins as well. You decide which pills you take."

"Thanks." I reach for the door and run out of the urgent care.

———

I give the pharmacy a few hours to fill my new prescriptions. I take a walk on the beach and feel like shit the entire time I'm there.

Mark's Pharmacy is empty when I stop in to pick up my new prescriptions. I'm not sure if Mark is the guy in the white coat behind the counter, but he looks at me, judgingly. A medical professional with a name like Mark should be a little more approachable.

"I'm going to assume you'll take one or the other." He rings up the prescriptions. "One-hundred and thirty-five dollars and ninety cents."

I pay cash.

On my way out I run into a tall man looking at the gum selection. I drop my bag. "Sorry." I tuck the pharmacy bag in my pocket.

"No problem." The man smiles at me awkwardly.

My eyes fall to the beating pulse in his neck. I lick my lips and force my gaze to his face. He's handsome in a southern manly man kinda way. He was probably one of those guys that had a stash of guns, booby-trapped property, and a boatload of survival food. Maybe that's why he's so awkward. Too much time alone. Be nicer, Meg. I smile back at him because that's what normal people do.

He opens his mouth like he's going to say something but turns and walks away instead. Weird. The Zombie Apocalypse really ruined social interactions here.

SKEELE

Skeele knew the moment Meg entered the pharmacy. He moved behind the shelving and pretended to look at soaps. He recounted the lessons Noah had given him before leaving Hell. *Don't be too pushy. Don't growl. Buy her some gifts. Take her to dinner.* It was a lot of information and most of it fled him in the moment. His mind instantly went black because Meg looked tired and weak. Her skin was pale. Noah didn't tell him how to approach Meg if she was looking like absolute shit warmed over. Guilt tugged at Skeele. Meg needed blood; she'd clearly gone without since she'd escaped to the Earthen plane.

She got a bag from the back counter.

Skeele moved closer, ready to make his move. He didn't have any pickup lines and he wasn't sure he could charm her. She just didn't look in the mood to talk to anyone let alone a complete stranger.

Meg was walking toward the door. Skeele had to act fast. She looked distracted, her head down and focused on the floor as she walked. It was like she didn't want to be seen. He stepped into the aisle. Meg ran into him and dropped her bag. He bent to pick it up, but she was too quick. Skeele didn't know what to say so he smiled. He was happy to see her and a little stunned that he'd finally found her.

Skeele wanted to say something, but nothing would come out.

He walked away.

Meg left the pharmacy.

Skeele felt like an idiot. He watched her get into a Jeep and followed her. It would be a challenge following her on foot, but Perdido Key was small and now he knew what kind of car she drove.

Meg took a right onto Perdido Key Drive. Skeele followed her, trying his best not to run full speed and make a spectacle. The slow-moving traffic in Perdido Key was a blessing if Skeele had ever come across one in his life. He kept up with Meg's Jeep and hid behind a fence as she pulled into the driveway of a little beach house. It was cute, colorful, and bright; the complete opposite of the castle in the burning caves of Hell. When Meg got out of her SUV and went to the door, short shorts and tanned legs, Skeele thought she almost looked like she belonged here.

————

MEG

I need to stay awake. It's been three weeks now. Three weeks without fresh blood. And I can't remember the last time I slept. All I know is that no one has found me.

I stare at the pills Dr. Jordan gave me. I still haven't taken either of them. I rub my face. I need to do something else. The coffee isn't working anymore, and I can't think clearly.

This is Florida. Land of the free. Home of the crack-heads. There are other ways to keep my eyelids open. I wait until dark and leave my house on foot. I don't want anyone to know what my car looks like. I walk down the main road to the gas station near Theo Baars Bridge. I've seen some sketchy people there. I wait near the entrance to a 7-Eleven for some shifty looking shit.

A man with greasy hair and limited tooth count lingers on the opposite side of the gas station. I stare at him. He stares at me. I rub my nose. He walks over.

"Hey," he says.

"Hey."

"You looking for some C?"

"Yeah. I brought cash."

"You want C or rocks?"

"Just the C." I reach into my pocket and pull out a bundle of cash.

"Whoa. Not here." He glances behind us and past the gas pumps, then motions for me to follow him. *Whoosh-whoosh-whoosh.* All I can hear is his jugular pumping. I lick my lips and follow. I follow him to the darkest shadows behind the building. It smells like rotting garbage next to the dumpster. I hold back the gagging feeling. Urgency prickled my spine to get this over and done with.

He digs in his pocket and pulls out a baggie with white powder. "It's five hundred."

I count the cash and we make the deal.

"Are you always here?" I ask. "When I need more."

"Usually." Rotten teeth peek out from behind dry lips. The combination is revolting. How could I ever think a Hellion was disgusting after looking at this specimen of humanity?

I leave the gas station and jog home.

I open the front door, slam it closed, and dig the baggie out of my pocket. I hold it up to the light. White crystals sparkle in the fluorescence. I've tried a lot of things and done a lot of awful shit, but this, this is me turning a new leaf. The coffee isn't working. I need to stay awake. I can't get found by Nightingale or the others.

I walk to the kitchen, dip my finger into the baggie and rub the white powder on my gums just like I've seen all those detectives do on TV.

Not only do I not sleep, but I also have so much energy that I clean the entire house by the time the sun rises. The toilets are scrubbed, every tile in the shower is sparkling. I can do it. I can do this and stop whenever I want. Whenever I get this thing out of my womb.

I stand in front of the bathroom mirror and turn sideways. I rub my hand over my stomach. It doesn't look any bigger. It's nice and flat and bikini ready. No one will ever know.

After looking at myself in the bathroom mirror for a few more minutes, I conclude I look like shit. The dark circles under my eyes look like they belong on a raccoon. My skin is pale, my hair dull. I slap my cheeks, but no redness appears. I need more bloody steaks, but I can't be going into the grocery store looking like the dead. I head to Mark's Pharmacy to get some makeup.

I lean down to look in the makeup aisle mirror with a handful of options. All the lipsticks look too bright and too pink against my pale skin. The foundations are too dark. I find a foundation that says "Snow" and rub it on the back of my hand. Jeeze, if snow is my color, then I'm beyond pale. I've never known myself to be this pale. I'm in Florida for God-sakes. I've spent half the week on the beach. I should have a sun-kissed glow by now.

I throw Snow into my basket and then grab another foundation that's two shades darker. Maybe I'll fake my color. Same with the lip colors. I decide on Dusty Rose and Carnation Mauve. Hopefully one of them will bring life back to my lips. I search for bronzer next.

As I'm walking down the aisle, inspecting my options, I get the feeling I'm being watched. I glance out of the corner of my eye and notice a tall man in jeans and button up shirt lingering nearby. I recognize him from the other day.

"Can I help you?" I ask.

"Hi, my name's Kal." He holds out his hand to shake.

I want to be annoyed but there's something so innocent and happy about the guy. I'm not one for shaking strangers' hands but this guy seems like he needs the greeting. "Meg," I say as I shake his warm hand, noticing the tattoos of pine trees snaking up his forearms.

"That's a nice name. Hey, would you like to go to dinner tonight?" he asks.

"Whoa buddy. Straight to the point."

"Sorry," he lets out an awkward sigh. "I know you don't know me, but I've seen you here a few times and you're always alone."

"You assumed I was single?"

"Kinda."

His smile is friendly, and he has a good vibe. I've been here alone, no friends, no boyfriends for weeks. Some socializing might do me some good. Some socializing might do him some good. I'm not one for picking up charity cases but what else do I have to do? I've completely failed at staying hidden in my new home. I might as well embrace leaving the house now.

"Well, Kal," I check him out. "You are correct. I'm single and ready to mingle. Where do you want to meet?" I head for the self-checkout and start scanning my items.

"Lady's choice."

"Oyster Bar near the bridge?" The place looks like it would have good food and I nearly don't care what the food tastes like as long as they have orange soda.

"Great. Six?" He looks at his watch.

"Six is good." I head for the door.

"I can walk you to your car." He skips ahead of me and holds the door open.

Damn, chivalry is not dead with this guy. No one has held a door for me since I got here. The Earthen plane has a bit to learn from Kal.

"The sun is so bright today." Kal pulls a pair of sunglasses from his pocket and puts them on as he follows me to my car.

"Sometimes it gives me headaches. I just have to close all the blinds and hide indoors." I want to say that I miss the ochre dimness of Hell. But that's not a conversation I can have on the Earthen plane.

I unlock my doors and notice the clouds collecting over the Gulf of Mexico. "What if it rains at six?" I ask.

"Neither of us should melt."

Kal opens my door. I get in and roll down the window as he closes the door. "We can meet at the restaurant."

"Do you do this a lot?" I ask.

"What?"

"Pick up strangers at the store. What if I'm a serial killer or a vampire or batshit crazy?"

Kal shrugs like it's no big deal. "Met a few of those. You don't fit the bill."

"You met a serial killer, a vampire, or a batshit crazy chick?"

"All the above." He looks at the clouds over the ocean. "I'd still like to meet you for dinner even if it rains."

"Okay," I say. "But I've warned you."

I start the Jeep and drive away. I watch Kal watching me in the rearview mirror. He looks like he just won the goldfish in the ball toss game at the summer carnival. Poor sucker.

———

SKEELE

His first lie was his name. Kal is innocent enough, but Skeele would rather shake some sense into Meg and drag her back to Hell where she belonged.

His second lie was telling Meg she didn't fit the bill of being a vampire or batshit crazy. She sure as shit fit the bill. But she had to be crazy to sit on that throne.

Skeele tugged his hat lower and started walking to the hotel. He was thinking about what he'd have to do if he scared Meg off. He listened to the ocean waves crash against the beach in the distance. For some this was very much a vacation, but Skeele found the sun too bright, the heat too hot, and the clothing too uncomfortable. And then there was the lack of free blood.

He passed a small house with a handwritten sign that said *For Rent*. Skeele stopped walking and considered. He couldn't stay at the hotel forever and if he wanted to invite Meg over, he needed a proper place to bring her too.

Skeele knocked on the door.

————

Meg

I walk the main road to the gas station near Theo Baars Bridge. I wait near the entrance to a 7-Eleven for my greasy-haired drug dealer. He shows up after ten minutes and motions for me to meet him around back.

Whoosh-whoosh-whoosh. I hear everyone's blood pumping. The drug dealer, the woman pumping gas, the teenager walking across the bridge. I try to focus on his mouth moving, I can barely hear him over the sound. *Whoosh-whoosh-whoosh.*

My dealer digs in his pocket. "Seven hundred."

"What?" I make a face. "That's more than last time."

He smiles, showing missing teeth. "This is how it works, sweetheart."

There's something about him, something slimy and fucked. *Whoosh-whoosh-whoosh.* I can't deal. Saliva fills my mouth. *Poof.* My teeth are on his neck, and I drain him of his blood in record time. It tastes better than anything I've had since arriving on the Earthen plane.

I drag his lifeless body down the ravine to the lagoon. I crouch so the cars passing can't see me. Wait. Wait. I check his pockets and pull out a handful of powder filled baggies from one pocket and a roll of cash from another pocket. Then I roll his body into the lagoon. The gators swim over immediately.

Standing, I back up into the shadows to calm down and take in my surroundings. No witnesses. Just the gators who seem more than happy with the free meal.

Poof.

I go back to my house and get ready for my date with Kal.

———

Skeele

Skeele checked his watch. Meg was seven minutes late. The hostess on the other side of the glass doors to the Oyster Bar was staring at him. It was making him uneasy. He glanced through the glass to find the hostess smiling at him. He bristled and tucked his hands in his pockets.

Meg's Jeep finally rolled into the parking lot of Oyster Bar and stopped in a parking space.

She was wearing jeans and a T-shirt. He would expect nothing less and was sure he'd never see her wear a dress again like the night of the celebration dinner.

The only difference in her outfit than what she typically wore in Hell was the flip-flops on her feet. Her toenails were painted black.

Skeele walked across the parking lot to meet her halfway. "I was afraid you weren't coming," he said.

Meg smiled and Skeele noticed the layers of makeup on her face.

"Are you feeling okay?" he asked. "You look tired."

"Gee, thanks," Meg had a sarcastic tone, but her eyes were hidden behind sunglasses.

"I didn't say it to be mean. We can reschedule."

"Nope," Meg said. "I'm hungry."

They crossed the stone parking lot. Skeele jogged ahead of Meg when they got to the door. He held it opened and ushered her inside with his hand on the small of her back.

Her T-shirt was cropped short, and his fingers pressed against Meg's warm skin. He wanted to touch more, but he was trying to be a gentleman.

He wanted to ask her why she left him drained of blood and with blue balls in her bed. But he was trying to lie about his identity.

Meg was staring out the window at the shore birds as they pecked the grass.

"What are you thinking about?" Skeele asked. "You seem like you're a million miles away."

Meg pointed to the white bird with stick legs. "I'm trying to decide if that's a Snowy Egret or White Ibis." She leaned closer to the window. "The ibis has a pink face. The egret has a yellow patch around their eyes. I can't tell the colors from here."

"Can I get you some drinks to start with?" a perky waitress with red bangle bracelets asked.

"Rum and coke," Meg said. "And an orange soda."

"Beer. Whatever you have on tap," Skeele said.

"I'll be back for your orders in a minute." The waitress paused to stare at Skeele.

"Bye now," Meg broke the waitresses longing over her date.

"Why are you so interested in the birds?" Skeele asked Meg.

Meg signed and ran her fingers through her short hair. "They bring me back to a simpler time." She toyed with her fork. "Remind me of old friends."

Skeele knew. He'd been there for the birdwatching. And he wondered if he was included in the old friends comment or if he was simply just a sack of blood for her to use at will.

———

MEG

I try not to think about my friends in Hell. It's better not to think about them since they are better off without me. Noah has his family. Skeele can move on to whatever life he had before I showed up and ruined it.

I cross my legs and try to quell the ache there. It started the moment Kal put his hand on my back, the second he touched my skin. I'll be damned if it's not the bloodlust rearing its ugly head. I've been so good. So, so good. It's been weeks. I'm surprised I didn't fuck a log after I drained my drug dealer. Somehow locking myself in my house prevented that. But now I'm here with a hot-blooded man who doesn't really seem like my type, but could be. I'm starting over, turning a new leaf. Maybe my type is Kal now. He's nice to look at, even if his head is close shaven and he always wears a baseball cap and seems a bit too nice.

I can't deny feeling better since having fresh blood. It's not like Skeele's, but close, close enough for a starving girl who survives on blood but tries her darndest to ignore that fact.

Kal orders steak. Rare with a side salad and French fries. I order shrimp fettuccini Alfredo. I skip the salad and get mozzarella sticks.

Kal asks me about the rest of the day, and I lie to him and say I walked on the beach and read a book.

"What book did you read?" Kal's eyes light up.

What a dork. I guess it's not the worst thing to get excited about.

"A Marilyn Monroe memoir."

Our food shows up and we chit-chat about Florida and the weather and what we do for work. I find it odd that we are both independently wealthy and don't have jobs. But times are different now on the Earthen plane. I read in a magazine that insurance companies had a heck of a payout to plenty of survivors. Being eaten by a zombie didn't fall under any act of God so they had to pay up on all their policies. Most of the survivors had large payouts. Kal's situation is probably one of them.

"Do you ever think of working?" Kal asks. "There's a blood bank across the bridge that's hiring."

I pause, a large forkful of pasta near my mouth. "I don't think that's a good idea."

Kal shrugs. "I thought about doing it to pass the time." He tips his empty glass at the waitress, and she brings him a new beer. "You know what they say, idleness is the devil's home for temptation."

"Do you all want dessert?" the waitress asks as she sets Kal's fresh beer down.

"Chocolate cake," I say. "With ice cream."

"And you?" she looks longingly at my date. I want to kick her in the ankle and tell her to get her own man. This hunk of awkward bookish flesh is mine. At least until I scare him away or kill him. With my record both are an option.

———

We watch the evening clouds thicken. Lightning illuminates the thunderheads over the Gulf.

"I like watching this." Kal points to the clouds. "The weather has never been like this anywhere I've lived."

"It's nice to watch until the lighting strikes too close." I push my chair back. "We should probably get going or we're going to get doused."

Kal stands and throws a few large bills on the table for the bill. He waves to the waitress and thumbs toward the stack of bills.

I didn't count what he left but I'm guessing he overpaid.

As we make our way to the front door, raindrops start falling.

"Where did you park?" I ask.

"I walked."

"You want a ride home?"

"Sure."

We run across the parking lot. Kal opens the driver side door and touches my back as I get in. It feels good. Skin against skin. Tingly. I know it's the blood lust talking but I can't ignore it. Kal slams the door and runs to the passenger side. The rain downpours, soaking him. Kal gets in.

"You barely made it," I say, starting the Jeep. "I think I have a towel back here." I turn and stretch to the back seat, reaching for the towel. Every good Floridian keeps a towel in the car for the summer rainy season. Usually, the wind will turn your umbrella inside out. It's better to run for cover and dry off after.

I feel warm fingers touch the skin on my side, his fingertips just skimming, making my spine tingle. Jesus. Why is he touching me like that?

"What?" I ask, dragging the towel and tossing it to Kal.

"You have a bruise on your hip." Kal dries his face with the towel. He pulls his wet shirt away from his body.

"You can take it off." I back out of the parking spot and head for Perdido Key Drive. "I hate sitting in wet clothes."

Kal tugs his shirt off and dries his neck and chest. His elbow knocks me in the shoulder. The guy is too big for the SUV.

"Sorry." He touches my shoulder, the one with the Scar from Sparrow's blade. I wince. "I didn't mean to do that."

I bite my lip and hold in a sound that wants to come from deep in my throat. This dude is too touchy and there was a time that I'd rather punch a man than let him touch me this much. But the bloodlust doesn't care about my feelings; it's soaking up every touch, every glance, every flirting tip of his lips. Oh my God what's wrong with me? I used to be so strong and edgy. Now I'm ready to melt like a long-haired blonde woman on the front of a romance novel.

I never ask Kal where he lives. Instead, I drive him to my house. I consider pulling off onto a dead-end road to bone him in the jeep. I still might. We've got a few more minutes before I have to turn onto Parasol Place. He doesn't say anything, he doesn't give me directions. The energy in the Jeep is tingly and hot and if I didn't know better, he doesn't want to go home. He's no better than me. Maybe that's the way it is here now. After nearly dying, all the survivors are horny and lonely.

The rain has turned into a deluge, ponding the streets and putting a hurt on my windshield wipers. It's the kind of white-knuckled driving no one talks during. I decide not to pull off onto a dead-end road because I can barely see the road.

I turn onto Parasol Place and park in my driveway.

"You want some coffee?" I glance at Kal's naked upper body. He must work out.

"Coffee sounds great." He reaches for the door handle, jumps out and rounds the Jeep to open my door. He holds the towel over our heads as we dash to the front porch.

Lightning strikes nearby, electrifying the air.

"Does that happen a lot here?" Kal asks as I search for

my house key. He rubs his arms, no doubt the nearby light-ning making his hair stand up.

"The lightning? Florida has the most lightning strikes out of anywhere." I shrug. "It happens."

"We better get inside." Kal rubs his arms with the towel then drapes it across my back and dries my neck.

That's it.

I shove the door open, grab him by the wrist to pull him inside, then slam the door closed.

"You are very flirty," I say, locking the door and invading his personal space.

He smiles, slowly, while looking down at me. His back is pressed against the door and my arm touches his side as I turn the lock.

Kal touches my chin, tips my face up to meet his, and puts his hands on me. He doesn't need to ask how far I want to go on the first date because I'm a grown ass woman and I'm already unbuttoning his jeans. The warmth of his lower abdomen seeps into my knuckles as I work the buttons.

"You want coffee first?" he asks, his hand moving into my hair and tugging my head back.

"Fuck the coffee." I kick off my flip-flops and reach for the hem of my crop top. If we were in Hell, I'd be able to use the bloodlust as an excuse for acting like a ho. But on the Earthen plane, there's no good excuse for taking Kal to my bed after one date.

Kal touches me everywhere. His big hands grip my breasts, his tongue licks my neck before his warm lips kiss down my chest. His hands slide into the waistband of my jeans, and he tugs them down. I kick them away.

"You're not wearing underwear," he whispers.

"I'm not apologizing for it." I tug at his jeans, trying to

control the urge to *poof* him to the bedroom and have my way with him.

His teeth nip my skin, and he grabs me by the waist, lifting me up onto the nearby countertop.

"Are you sure–" he starts to ask, only to be interrupted by my legs wrapping around him and pressing him into me.

———

I wake to the soft breathing of a large body in my bed. I roll to the side, my eyelids heavy, my legs sore. My eyes focus on the nightstand clock. It's three a.m.

Shit. Shit. Shit. Shit. I fell asleep.

Nausea sneaks up my stomach. I slide out of bed and run to the bathroom.

I hurl up the fancy dinner Kal bought me and wish for blood. The drug dealer's blood should have lasted me longer. All it did was make me horny. There were days when I fed from Skeele more than once, but this feels extreme.

I start the shower. A cold shower will wake me up really good. Then I'll make some coffee and watch a movie and think of a good lie to tell Kal for why I left him in my bed alone.

I notice the bruise on my hip. There's a new bruise on my thigh, but that was from Kal carrying me across the house while I did unlady-like things. I'm not sure how he walked while I did that. I lather and rinse and wash my hair and think about how he didn't seem to notice the birthmark on my upper thigh. Maybe men on the Earthen plane are no longer impressed with tattoos and scars and strange birthmarks.

———

The coffeemaker doesn't wake Kal. Neither does my cursing as I search the TV for a movie. I want to watch Shawshank Redemption like the good old days, but the only things playing are horror and teen dance movies. I settle on horror and hope to scare myself awake. I wrap myself in a blanket from the back of the couch and sip at my sugar and cream laden coffee. My stomach grumbles and I consider finding a snack since my dinner is gone. There's one last bloody steak in the fridge. I could eat that, but I don't want to risk Kal walking in on me as I eat raw meat like that old man on the beach.

Kal is standing in the doorway, watching me. "Are you hungry?" he asks. It sounds familiar. I'd like to say yes. I'd like to tell him I'm hungry for his blood and that I want to screw and bite his neck. But I'm on the Earthen plane now, and Kal is a normal guy, a nice guy.

"Do you want me to make something?" Kal asks. "Or do you want me to go?"

I glance at his nearly naked form, the bulge in his boxer-briefs. No, I don't want him to go. I can still feel the urge from the bloodlust. He should stay so I don't wind up fucking a log in the backyard. My new neighbors wouldn't enjoy witnessing that.

I lift the blanket and ask him to sit with me. Kal stretches an arm across my back, and I lay my head on his shoulder.

I blink and take a mental snapshot. I file it under *the way things could have been*. We could have been a sweet young couple who survived the Zombie Apocalypse and help repopulate the world. We could have been something normal and nice. Like dinners on Sunday evenings and weddings and first birthday parties and proms. But that will never be because I am the ruler of Hell and Kal is a normal guy. Even though this charade just started, it's going to need to end. If he stays in the picture, it won't end well. I don't want to feed him to the gators. That would be tragic.

Kal taps my hip with his hand. "Are you okay?" he asks.

"I'm fine." I stretch my hand across his bare chest and to his shoulder, up the side of his neck and stretch my fingers across the back of his head.

Kal groans and he tips his head just so. *Whoosh-whoosh-whoosh*. If I didn't know better, I'd take it as an invitation. I take it as an invitation for other things. I move to my knees and straddle his lap and curse the bloodlust for ever existing.

———

Noah, Jed, Nightingale, and Shay

"He's found her," Nightingale told the others at the table. "I didn't approach her in the dream. She hasn't slept in a long time."

"Let her sleep," Noah said, shifting a sleeping Thrush in his arms. There was a wet drool mark on his shoulder, but Noah ignored it.

"How long will it take Skeele to bring her back?" Shay asked. Jed was in the middle of updating the runes on her arms. Shay's blowtorch blue hair contrasted against her pale skin and dark clothing in a newly shortened haircut to her chin. Shay sucked in a breath as Jed tattooed deep over bone.

"Sorry," he said as his thumb rubbed her skin to soothe.

Nightingale and Noah made eye contact. Jed and Shay had spent every moment together since Thrush had his parents back. Now they were on standby. Guardians for

Thrush in case something happened to Nightingale or Noah again. Without Meg in Hell, there was bound to be some drama initiated by the Deacons. They didn't like that they had no control over Meg.

Rumors were starting. Someone had destroyed portals on the Earthen plane. The Deacons had already come knocking on the doors of the burning caves. Clea distracted them and sent them away. But it wasn't enough. The new Hellions had mouths that spoke freely at whatever post they were stationed. They were instructed to bring the rumors back to Klaus and Chel, but some had loose lips and spread their own rumors. The demons of Hell knew the throne was unseated. Meg wasn't as visible as she had been.

There was a knock on the door.

Nightingale moved to answer it. Chel, Klaus, and Tukka entered the room. Suddenly the chapel in the cemetery felt very small.

Klaus was carrying a bag. "This should be everything."

Nightingale took the bag as Jed stopped his tattooing, wiped Shay's skin, and rubbed a layer of healing balm over the fresh ink.

"Are you ready?" Jed asked Shay.

Shay nodded and stood.

Tukka grunted in disapproval. "They are nothing alike. This will not work."

Nightingale pulled clothing from the bag and held them up to Shay. "The clothes will fit."

"Her hair is blue," Tukka motioned to Shay's hair. "Meg's is black. Everyone will know it's not her." He was agitated. "She doesn't even have Meg's tattoos."

"Or her attitude," Klaus said with a smile, trying to lighten the mood.

"Hush, all of you." Noah patted Thrush's back,

soothing him to sleep again. "She has a few of the tattoos. Jed still has time to add more."

"Here," Nightingale thrust the clothing into Shay's hands. "Go change."

"Come with me." Shay tugged at Jed's shirt as she headed to the bedroom.

Shay closed the door behind Jed and listened to the chatter in the living room.

"They don't want me to do this." Shay tossed the clothing onto the bed and kicked off her boots.

"It doesn't matter." Jed turned his back like a gentleman. "We have to do something until we can get Meg back where she belongs."

"What if she never comes back?" Shay asked. "I'm a human. I am not whatever magical creatures you all are. I don't have wings or magic or battle training."

"Meg doesn't have any of those either." Jed pressed his ear to the wooden door to hear the others speaking.

"She has something that keeps you all in check." Shay pulled on a pair of jeans that were a little too tight on the butt. She changed her shirt to the wide-necked blue T-shirt of Meg's. "Okay. Turn around. Tell me how bad this is."

Jed turned and walked a circle around Shay. "I think this could work." He stopped in front of Shay and frowned.

"It's the blue hair, isn't it?"

Jed shook his head in defeat. "Everyone knows you have the blue hair. We have to hide it."

"It took a really long time to get this shade just right." Shay was annoyed. "If you fuck it up..."

Jed's lip tipped to form a half smile. "Say it like Meg would."

Shay closed her eyes and took a deep breath, collecting

every speck of attitude and edge in her person. "If you fuck it up, I will drain you dry." Shay opened her eyes.

Jed was nodding in approval. "That was pretty good." He held out his hands and his fingers danced in rhythmic spellcasting. "Let's just add a little glamour so as not to fuck up your blue."

When Shay left the bedroom, the visitors in the living room were silent, judging, and one of them eating crow, figuratively.

"Fine," Tukka said, his tone dull. "But don't let anyone get too close to her. Meg has blue eyes."

"We will make sure," Klaus said, reaching for the door handle so they could leave.

Chel motioned for Shay to follow them. "After you, Queen of Hell."

———

Skeele

Skeele waited two days before inviting Meg out again. That's what Noah and the others had told him. *Don't seem desperate, give her distance, don't be overbearing.* All their dating advice ran through his head daily.

Skeele set his book down and walked to the small fridge to get a bag of blood. There were only two left. This was taking much longer than he'd planned. He thought about the blood bank on the other side of the Theo Baars bridge. If something didn't change soon, he'd be applying at that blood bank for a job. Soon.

Meg wanted to go to a dive bar on the water. The food was good, but she'd warn cutoff jean shorts and a tank top. Every man was looking at her and she didn't even realize it.

And Skeele figured the damn woman would walk around naked daily if she could. Possessiveness thrummed in his chest as he glared down a college kid at the bar. It took the guy entirely too long to stop looking at Meg's legs. If only these dudes knew what she would do to them.

Skeele did all the things; a light touch to her back, plenty of smiles, touched her hand as they talked, asked about her day. It wasn't hard to notice that underneath Meg's smiles she was hiding something.

She was thinner than ever and started wearing makeup to cover the blue crescents of fatigue under her eyes. Skeele didn't like it. He was sure she was trying to wean herself off the blood and that was why she was at the doctor's and the pharmacy so often. He'd heard her vomiting enough times and he was starting to think it wasn't because of her disgust of his Hellion form.

This night wasn't much different from the last night they were together. Meg invited him back for coffee. As things were getting hot and heavy in the kitchen Meg paused, covered her mouth, and ran to the bathroom.

Skeele heard her retching and went to the sink to get her a glass of water. Demons knew better than to deny themselves blood. Meg's battle was impossible; she'd never wean herself off the blood. He couldn't shake the feeling that this didn't make complete sense. She'd been denying herself fresh blood for a while-the vomiting started back in Hell. He remembered her cut arm. Maybe it's the poison working its way out? Skeele wasn't a healer, and he could only guess what was really going on with her. He just hoped he could convince her to go home as soon as possible.

Skeele set his hand on the countertop and felt something granular pressing into his skin. Skeele wiped the counter, fine white dust collected near his palm. He noticed a bag hiding behind the toaster and pulled it out. Skeele tasted it. This wasn't sugar or salt.

Suddenly it was starting to make sense. Her thinness, her lack of sleeping. Skeele wanted to slam a fist into the cabinets, but he didn't want to scare her. He pocketed the bag of white powder and went to the bathroom to help.

Skeele knocked on the door until Meg opened. He handed her the glass of water as she was putting toothpaste on a toothbrush.

"Thanks," Meg said.

"You want me to make something to eat?"

"Since I flushed my dinner down the toilet?" she asked. "Sure."

"What do you want?"

Meg thought for a minute. "Spaghetti."

Skeele wasn't much of a cook, but he figured he could handle spaghetti. He read the instructions on the box to make the pasta. After draining it and mixing it with jarred sauce from the pantry, Skeele had an idea. He took two bowls out of the cabinet and filled them, then he grabbed a knife from the drawer. He stood with his back to the hall where Meg was cleaning up and sliced his arm, dripping fresh blood into Meg's bowl of spaghetti.

"Smells good in here," Meg's voice broke the silence.

Skeele turned on the sink and rinsed off the knife. He licked his arm to seal the wound.

"Hey, just in time," he said as he stirred Meg's dinner, mixing the blood into the sauce.

"I'm starved," she said, taking the bowl and sitting on the couch.

———

MEG

Kal can cook. I've never tasted a bowl of spaghetti so delicious.

"What did you do to this sauce?" I ask.

"Poured it out of the jar," Kal says. "You think it's good? I've never made it before."

I stare like a weirdo. "You've never cooked spaghetti before? Have you even lived?"

He laughs nervously and rubs a hand over his head. "I mean, I've had spaghetti before, I just don't cook it. It's one of those things. Have you made cheesecake?"

I shake my head.

"See. Some things we only buy."

I get up to clean and reach for Kal's empty bowl. "You want more?" I ask.

Kal gets up and follows me. "No. I'm full. Two dinners are enough for me."

"Apparently not for me." I set the bowls in the sink and turn on the water. I notice a splash of red on the side of the sink.

"I'll clean up later." Kal turns me and touches my neck. "You sure?"

"There are better things to do right now." His eyes drop to my lips and heat spreads across my abdomen. Suddenly I feel like I'm in the tormented state of bloodlust. That spaghetti must've been magical. Maybe it was the act of a man taking care of me. Maybe that's what did it. He takes off his shirt and reaches for mine.

We make it to the couch again. Kal sucks in a breath as I lean into him and press my teeth to his neck. I want to break the skin. I want to bite hard and taste the blood. But I don't because Kal is human and I'm on the Earthen plane. And I'm trying to do better.

Kal's hands tighten on my hips then he jerks me down onto his hardness. "Yes, my night owl," his voice is low. The words sound more like a muttering, like a secret he wants to keep to himself instead of share with me, like a prayer to the darkness, a mantra to the night. I get the feeling those words weren't meant for me to hear. Perhaps they were meant for someone else, not a fling after a few nights. Kal's probably using me to forget someone else. I can't say I haven't done that before.

My night owl. I kiss his neck instead of draining him dry and I consider, as our bodies move together, languid and slow, maybe I should leave Kal so I don't hurt him like I've hurt the rest of my friends. He deserves better than what I'll do to him. I'll break him. I'll burn him. I just might lose control and kill him. The urges have been harder to contain, after all.

And, like he hears my thoughts, his arms pull me close, wrapping tightly and rolling us until I am below him, taking his weight and thrusts as he kisses me, whispers on my lips, "Stay."

I must be easy to read; in the short time we've been together Kal can sense I'm ready to run away.

Skeele

Skeele didn't know the glamour translated his Hellspeak. He didn't know Meg finally heard what he had been calling her all those nights she took him to her room. All those nights he promised on his honor to serve her without getting attached.

He couldn't ignore she had that look the veil of night could not hide. That same look she got when she was ready to run. He'd seen it before, felt the pulling away. He reminded himself that she was feral and wild. *Don't get attached*. He could be loyal and serve her throne as he'd promised.

The bloodlust was her addiction. He knew how to keep her focused and present, a little blood, a bit of his body, and she'd stay for a few moments longer. It was manipulative. He knew that but it was for her safety. Meg was running from herself, and Skeele was taking his time on the Earthen plane since the Deacons wanted his hide in retribution.

MEG

I decide to spend my day at the beach and take a break from Kal. I haven't had blood in a week, and being around him is getting dangerous. I wanted to sink my teeth into his neck the other night. If I know anything about myself, I'll lose control and do it. Then I'll have a mess to clean up. This is why I left Hell, being a danger to others is no fun at all. It's better to be alone.

The bag of C is missing from behind my toaster. Either Kal found it, or I can't remember moving it. Not that this would be the first time I can't remember what I've done. It's happened before. I'd like to think Kal didn't touch it. He's too good to do something like that.

I walk in the tide, my footprints sinking in the sand. I decide when I get home, I'm going to take the morning after pill that Dr. Jordan prescribed me. I think that's the best option for me.

I walk a good few miles before I notice the cooler breeze. Beachgoers are leaving in droves. Soon, I'm the only one left and my walk home is peaceful: nothing but the sound of the waves and the thunder rolling in.

There's a single man lying on his stomach facing the ocean, reading, and watching the storm clouds form. I'd recognize that ass anywhere. It's Kal. So much for avoiding him.

"Hey," Kal moves to his feet. It's a sight for sore eyes. He's ripped and slightly tanned and fills out his board shorts perfectly. He's too perfect. I could eat him whole but then I'd be sad that he would be dead.

"Hey," I wave and walk toward him.

"This water is amazing," he motions to the turquoise water of the Florida panhandle. "I've seen nothing like it." He pauses, his head tips. "What's that?"

Kal raises his arm; the hairs stand on edge. He reaches forward and touches my hair.

"It's sticking up all over the place," he says with a little laugh.

Oh no. I read about this in a safety pamphlet at the doctor's office. Static energy fills the air. BAM! A bright burst of light explodes around us.

Somebody That I Used To Know

The Deacons

The Deacons couldn't leave a Hellion lying unconscious on a beach in the Earthen plane. Especially with the glamour shocked out of him. He had runes to hide him, but a Hellion was a Hellion and the naked eye saw what it saw. There was no hiding now that the ruler of the Earthen plane had called them out with a bolt of electricity.

There is really one entity that keeps the world running. The cleanup crew. The scavengers, the vultures, the worms and dung beetles. The Deacons do the same for the realms. The cleaners, the scrapers. The Deacons make sure every soul has time to repent. Heaven or Hell is a choice, the Earthen plane a playground. But there were rules as old as the beginning of time that have waned and wavered. Rules for balance and rules for retribution. And, there was the simple fact that the Deacons favored the Seven Kingdoms of Heaven, although Meg had seen that firsthand. It wasn't a surprise to her. But times were changing, realms were shifting, the fast-Zombie War brought forth transformation; not just in the Seven Kingdoms of Heaven but the Earthen plane as well. The Deacons had seen the change in Hell with Meg at the throne. They kept close tabs as her kingdom grew by leaps and bounds. Plenty had died in the fast-Zombie War, plenty had woken in Hell, plenty had left the Safe Houses without ever ascending. Suddenly, Hell wasn't such a bad ending for many.

Skeele and Meg lay unconscious on the beach. The lightning strike left matching Lichtenberg figures in fernlike scars down their back and arms, mirroring each other. Whereas a human's scars from such an event would be red, theirs were blacker than any ink. Scorched to their bones, it was a message left to be interpreted in a variety of ways. But predominantly as, Stay Out!

Meg had been told there was no God and many times she'd formed her own conclusion that a true being was not there, but an energy was. That's the only explanation for how she found Sparrow so quickly. Now that energy wanted Meg and Skeele out of his realm. Or perhaps, it could no longer stand by and witness Meg's self-destruction.

The Deacons arrived in record time. They scooped the two bodies off the sand and walked them into the ocean. They moved calmly and with ease. The one carrying Skeele's giant body lifted him as if he were no more than a child's size. Each Deacon chanted the same phrase that turned the water into a portal and brought them to a Safe House.

———

MEG

I never thought I'd see this room again. The desk opposite me draws up feelings that I'd rather not experience. Last time I sat in this chair, I did not know what I was. I was nothing but a wandering soul on the wrong plane looking for trouble.

"Tell us what happened," the man from the center of the desk-of-questioning says to me.

"Nothing happened. I was walking on the beach and got struck by lightning." I rub my sweaty palms across my white scrubs.

"Something definitely happened," the one on the right says.

I press my lips together. I'm not answering to these fucks. I'd kill everyone in this room if I could.

"You should take better care of yourself in your condition," the one on the left says.

"My condition? What's wrong with my condition?" I ask, crossing my arms.

He presses his lips together before looking at his friends. "Let's start with the drugs."

"Lots of people do drugs." I shrug, annoyed. "No biggie."

"In your condition?" the one in the center says. "Do you realize what you could have done?"

"My condition is fine. Tip top shape." Nausea rolls up the back of my throat, but I swallow it down. I won't let my body show them I am a liar. I haven't had much control over myself these past few months, but this instant I will.

I should have taken that pill the day Dr. Jordan wrote for it. I should have ended this immediately. Never once did I think the thing in my belly would put a target on my back.

"You know," I cross my arms, "I'm still unhappy that you never gave me back my guns last time I was here."

The men don't say a thing.

"I'd like to give this place zero stars." I hold up my index finger and thumb in a circle.

"That doesn't matter here," the man in the middle says.

"It should." I rub away the ache from the mark down my arm left by the lightning strike.

The one on the left waves toward me. "Maybe you should come back later, when you can tell the truth."

"Whatever you think is the truth is most likely wrong," I say.

"Sparrow told us–"

I stand. "Don't." I point at them. "Don't you dare. This is my realm. I rule here. I am truth. Sparrow knows nothing!" I grip the back of the chair. "Let me the fuck out of here now!" I pick up the chair and throw it at the men. The chair hits their desk and falls to the ground. The men sit still, unscathed, unshocked, uncaring.

The one on the right waves to a Deacon near the door. If everything runs like the last time I was here, this is my Parole Officer. Poor schmuck. They assigned this Deacon to take me back and forth and hear me repent. I'm not sure if this is like regular Containment, because I'm not just any prisoner. I've noticed a few things: Newcomers wear maroon scrubs and they put me in white. I never got my Qualifiers checklist, an intake form where we write all the information we can remember and our greatest sins. Nope, they must've saved mine from last time I was here. The sins are the same. I'd probably need an additional sheet or two to include everything now.

The Deacon walks me back to my cell. "You'll be safe here. Safer than you've been out there."

"Shut up," I seethe.

The Deacon's mouth snaps closed, and he looks uneasy. The first time I was here, I thought they were helpful and kind, but then they sent a Scarecrow after me and colluded with the Seven Kingdoms of Heaven. I've realized that they are not helpful or kind, simply prying and meddlesome. Maybe they help the lost souls repent and guide them to where they need to go, but when it comes to me, they've brought nothing but trouble.

Prisons are all set up similar. They have me in a basement, no windows. I think it's solitary confinement. Probably for the better. They can't risk putting me in with the others. What an influence I would be on the newly dead.

There's a six-pack of Ginger Ale on my bed.

"The kitchen sent it," the Deacon says. "For your upset stomach."

"My stomach is fine."

"Uh hm." The Deacon opens the door to my cell.

I wander inside and he slams it closed like I am some dangerous criminal.

I've tried not wandering inside after Deacon opens my cell door. I've tried faking him out and running in another direction. I didn't get far. I can't walk through bars of iron, and I don't know the layout of this prison. Truth is, I'll run into a wall before I find a door. No, I can't run screaming down the halls. I have to be smart. I have to watch them and plan my escape. Just like last time.

The Deacon leaves with a jingle of his keys. I turn on the sink and splash water on my face, trying not to puke. I don't want him to hear me. My hands shake under the stream of water as I splash it and rub my face and neck. I'm not sure if it's the thing in my belly or the lack of C making me feel like absolute shit. Maybe it's the food here? I grab a ginger ale, crack it open, and sip.

I'm not sure how long I've been here. I was out for a while after the lightning strike on the beach. I would have thought living through that would have taken care of things. Seems it didn't. Hell, I wouldn't know. I need a meeting with Teari so she can answer all my questions. Poor Kal, though. I'm sure he's deader than a doornail.

I settle on the bed, put my hands behind my head, and cross my ankles. Since I have nothing better to do than wait for dinner, I take a nap. Maybe Nightingale will find me since she enjoys snooping so much.

My nap doesn't last long. Something roars like a wild animal from a few cells down. I sit up in bed. I thought I was alone. I stand and move to the bars, gripping them, pressing my face against the metal to see what's happening.

There's four Deacons in the hall. They're carrying electric batons; I can hear the static zapping. Scuffling ensues, slaps and punches echo. The Deacons are yelling at someone.

I wait, holding my breath to see who walks by. A giant form shuffles and shoves. I'd recognize those horns anywhere.

"Skeele!" I shout. He's cuffed and electrified batons threaten to zap him from all sides as he walks. He sneers, his eyes filled with hate like a wild animal trapped in a zoo.

I reach out from between the bars only for a Deacon to slap my arm away. The motion shoves my injury from Sparrow's blade into the bars.

"Ow," I shout, "You don't have to be such a dick. Just let me talk to him! Skeele!"

They don't let me talk to him, they take him away and he doesn't even seem to recognize me.

Maybe he's mad? I'd be mad at me for leaving like I did. I never said goodbye, I just disappeared. I never told him about... damn.

Shay and Jed

Shay stood in the middle of Meg's room feeling uneasy. "This seems so wrong," she said.

Jed was brushing crushed bird seed off the balcony railing.

"What's this?" Shay picked up the jar of mottled feathers from Meg's bedside table.

"I'm not sure," Jed said as he walks into the room. "But judging from the scarce decorations in this room, if it's here then it's important to her."

Shay set the jar down and wandered around the room, then the closet, then the bathroom. "Do I have to stay in here?" she asked. "It really feels like a violation of her privacy."

Jed followed Shay. "Look, we are doing her a favor."

"No one will know." Shay made her way to the balcony for some fresh air.

Jed stood next to her, scanning the tree line. He saw movement and pointed it out to Shay. "That creature would know if this room were empty."

Shay leaned forward and squinted. "What is it?"

"Probably a demon."

"You don't think it's Demore?" Shay asked.

Jed shook his head. "It's too early in the night for Demore." He took a piece of sharp charcoal from his jacket pocket and began sketching runes of protection on the balcony railing. "It could be another Deacon."

"Meg drinks blood," Shay said. "Are they going to want me to drink blood?"

"You don't have to drink blood. You're human."

There was a cry off in the forest. It sounded like an animal or a bird. But Jed and Shay knew it could be something else.

Shay's breasts felt warm as milk letdown.

"Ugh." Shay touched her chest and felt wetness. "Is this ever going to stop?" She knew it could go on for weeks while her milk dried up. Now that Nightingale was back, Thrush didn't need a wet-nurse.

Jed touched her arm. "Come inside, I'll help you with that."

———

NIGHTINGALE

Nightingale sat in creaking rocking chair. Thrush tucked against her chest.

"How long will you be like this?" Noah asked.

Nightingale smiled. "Forever." She kissed her baby. "Forever and ever."

Noah flashed from one side of the room to the other. "We can stay like this?" He knelt beside her. "No more sneaking off to the Astral to be together?"

"No."

"And Thrush?"

"Will grow and find his place. Then it will just be us."

Noah dropped his head. "I never thought we'd be

together again." He paused for a moment. "What about Jack?"

"He's gone." Nightingale looked away, remembering the ambush during the fast-Zombie War. "He went wherever I went. The only thing that brought me back was Thrush."

Noah nodded, solemn. He reached out and touched Nightingale's cheek, the scars that marred her skin.

Nightingale turned away. "Don't." She wasn't ready to deal with the scars and what had happened. She only wanted to revel in the joy of having her baby in her arms again.

"Will you search for Meg tonight?" Noah asked. "I feel like there's something very wrong."

Nightingale stopped rocking. "What's wrong?"

"I lost my connection to her when she left, but for some reason," Noah paced and ran his hands through his hair. "For some reason I feel like she's nearby."

Nightingale stood and took Thrush to his crib. She lay him down gently and patted his back until he was deep asleep. She left the nursery and closed the door.

"You think she's here in Hell?" Nightingale asked Noah. "Skeele didn't bring her back to us."

"I know. There's still a connection though, weak but there. She's back on this plane."

Nightingale made her way to the bedroom. "I guess we better find out where she is then."

———

MEG

I wish I could *poof* out of here. But the lightning strike did something to me. I trace the marks on my arm. I was a complete idiot for releasing Noah from our tether. If I'd never done that, I could summon him to this place. He'd be able to find me in an instant and help set me free. It's better this way. I've had to rely on myself my whole life before. There's no difference now. The more I think of it, the more I realize I've been around too many people. My inner circle is much too large. I need to shrink it down to one. Single. That's the best way to do things. Look what happened to poor Kal.

I fluff the flat pillow under my head by beating it with my fists. It doesn't do much. The pillow has the fluff of a piece of cardboard.

"Breakfast," a Deacon slides a tray into my cell.

I get up and see what they brought me.

More slop and plastic silverware. I sit on the floor and lean against the bed while I eat the cold oatmeal with strange milk and a brown banana. Either the food budget is tight or they're punishing me by way of my stomach. The food was strange last time I was here. Unpasteurized milk that stunk and odd meats.

My shirt catches on something sharp. Peeking from under the mattress, tucked between the spring and metal frame, is a tarnished metal spoon. Anything metal is a prize when you're locked in a cell like this. This thing looks old. I hold it in my hand and rub my thumb over the smooth handle.

Last time I dug my way out of jail, I had to steal the spoon myself from the galley. Those were the days.

"Hey," I whisper down the hall.

Skeele doesn't answer.

"Hey, are you there?" I ask again.

This is probably a bad time to shout between the bars

that I've got a fetus in my belly and it's his. That seems insensitive and I've been enough of a jerk to Skeele. I've got to tell him sometime and we need to get out of here.

I pace in my cell and think of a plan. I rub my fingers on the spoon, fidgeting. I crawl across the bed and hang my bedsheet along the back wall and make it look like I'm just a slob who doesn't make their bed in the morning. If I dig under the bed, the sheet could hide it. I leave it like that to see if anyone notices throughout the day.

The doors squeal. Metal on metal. Plenty of footsteps follow. Four Deacons walk by dragging Skeele. There's blood dripping down his back, a trail streaks across the floor. Thick and coagulated. My mouth waters.

I move to the bars like a starved lioness. "Skeele!" I shout. "What did you do to him?"

No one answers. The Deacons don't look at me.

After they leave, I reach out and touch the streaks of blood on the floor. I collect some on my fingertip and smell it. Damn. Saliva fills my mouth. I lick the blood off my fingers and reach out for more. I move across the front bars of my cell, scooping as much of the streaks as I can reach. It's disgusting. Dirty. It tastes so good. I miss his blood.

"What did they do to you?" I finally ask, hoping he'll answer.

He doesn't.

I lick the redness from between my fingernails, I close my eyes and try to poof; nothing happens. That lighting strike really fucked with my ability to travel at will.

———

Rolling over in the squeaking bed, a spring pokes me in the back. I open my eyes and hold my hand over my mouth. I take three deep breaths, hoping it will pass.

"You feeling okay?" My Deacon is here, prying eyes and imploring tone.

"Never better." I lie. "Tip-top."

"Be ready in thirty minutes. You're going to Questioning again today."

"Joy."

Another Deacon brings me a tray of food and slides it through the access near the door. I eat some of the toast while I get ready. There's not much to do. I don't want to wear my dirty clothes, so I keep wearing the white scrubs they bring me each day. I wash my face and scrub my neck. Then I wait until my Deacon returns.

I stand at the bars and press the side of my face against them, trying to see down the hall to the cell where Skeele is being kept.

"Hey," I whisper. "Hey, are you there?"

A grunt replies.

"What did they do to you?" I ask.

The Archangels tore up my back once before. I'm surprised the Deacons would employ similar methods of punishment. I've never seen them hurt a person before. While they've meddled and gotten people hurt, I've never seen them deliver a punishment.

The thirty minutes goes by fast. Deacon collects me from my cell for more questioning. It's always the same questions. I'm tired of it.

"Come on, Meg." Deacon motions for me to leave the cell.

"What did you do to Skeele?" I ask, crossing my arms and standing my ground.

"That's not open for discussion." He motions again. "Time to go."

"I don't want to go. I want to know what happened to him."

Deacon leans forward and lowers his voice. "We know you licked his blood off the floor."

I swallow down my shame. "So? It's what I am. You know that."

"It means something."

"Yeah. It means I'm hungry for more than the slop you've been bringing me every day. What do I have to do to get a rare steak or a bag of blood in this joint?"

Deacon smiles. "Let's go."

"Skeele?" I shout and run for the hall.

Deacon grabs me. He's strong, but after that little bit of fresh blood, I'm stronger. I tear myself away from him and run down the hall to Skeele's cell.

His large form is lying on the bed, his torn up back on display. His arms and wings hang over the bed and drape on the floor. He looks entirely too large for the cell and the furnishings. He's not moving.

"What did you do to him?" I snap.

"He'll be fine. He's a big boy."

"No one deserves that." I reach into the cell but he's too far away. I want to shake him awake to make sure he's okay.

"If you knew, you might change your mind," my Deacon replies with a sarcastic tone.

I glare at Deacon and consider injuring him. I might be able to do it. I can't *poof* from here to there, but I have a spec of extra energy from the blood. I'll probably have the blood lust soon too.

I grip the bars of Skeele's cell.

"You can't help him," Deacon says.

"Why not?" I argue.

"He's killed."

"He's a Hellion. It's his job," I say.

"All are forbidden from preventing Newcomers to Hell from reaching a Safe House to repent and find their place."

"He killed a Newcomer?" I ask. "He would never. Skeele is as straight as they come. All rules, no breaking them. It had to have been a mistake."

"It wasn't. Let's go. They're waiting for you."

———

In the night, I hear a strange noise; a cooing. I can't be too deep if there's an animal this close. I slide my arm behind the bed and chip away at the old cement. The old spoon works as well as can be expected. I barely hear the small pieces of cement falling to the floor. I work on digging for a few hours, until my fingers are numb and my arm is sore. When I'm satisfied with the hard night's work, I collect the small pile of cement chips and dust and put it in my pocket. The cooing noise stops not long before sunrise.

———

"Sundays are for visitors," Deacon says.

"No one knows I'm here."

"I think you'll be surprised to see who knows." He motions for me to move. "Come on. Might raise your spirits."

He walks me up three flights of stairs. The layout starts to look familiar. There are windows and more cells that turn into real hallways with solid doors. He opens the one that says *Visitation*.

Clea is waiting, sitting with her back straight and hands folded on her lap, still as stone.

"Child," she says as I enter. "It's been too long."

"How did you find me?" I ask as the Deacon leaves.

"A mother's tether is forever strong." She motions for me to sit with her eyes. "Nightingale has been looking also. She said you haven't been sleeping very well. She hasn't been able to invade your dreams."

I've missed her paleness and red lips, the way her figure wavers like she's about to flitter away to the Astral realm.

"What happened to your neck and arm?" she asks.

I hold up the arm with the dark marks. "Struck by lightning."

She stares, intensity in her eyes. "It's best you're here then."

The door opens and Skeele walks into the room. I step to the side to make space for him. He doesn't look so hot.

I hold back the feeling of excitement at finally seeing him in his semi-normal state.

Clea's expression turns concerned as she examines him from her seat. "You as well?" she asks him.

"What?" he asks.

"Your hand." Clea points.

Skeele is wearing the same white scrubs as me and since we've been here, I've only seen him in passing. Now, I see the marks on his hand and the side of his neck. Lightning scars, just like mine.

"What the fuck?" I say as I grab his wrist and pull his arm out straight. "How did you get those?"

Skeele doesn't answer. He makes a face like a kicked puppy.

"When I was on the Earthen plane, I was on a date at the beach with a nice guy named Kal. We both got struck by lightning," I say.

Skeele is silent.

"How the fuck did you get struck by lightning?" I hold up my arm against his. "Why do these scars match?" I tug at my shirt, showing him the blackened fern-like patterns that extend from my neck, down my chest, covering the disfigured Sparrow tattoo. "You're fucking Kal, aren't you?"

"You ran away," Skeele finally speaks.

I look at Clea for support but she's too busy watching us intently.

"You lied to me," I say.

"Yes."

"You hunted me."

"It wasn't hard." Skeele touches the marks on his hand, the forest tattoos on his forearms. "Jed taught me the glamour. If you are going to be mad, be mad at everyone. We were trying to bring you home."

"Don't tell me who to be mad at." I control the urge to attack like a rabid animal. I want to. My emotions are teetering on the edge.

"Child," Clea interrupts. "I'm bringing the others to see you. We have to figure out a way to get you out of here."

"I already have one." I whisper. "I've done this before."

Clea blinks.

"It was a bit of a different situation, but I figured it all out." I make a shoveling motion with my hand.

Clea makes a face. She doesn't understand and I just turn out looking stupid, jerking my hand around.

I lean forward. "I'm digging a tunnel."

"Come on," Skeele exhales a breath of exasperation.

"I'm halfway. I've done this before." I reach into my

pocket and pull out a handful of cement and dirt. "I'll be topside in a few weeks."

"We can't stay in here for weeks," Skeele rubs his horns.

"Regardless, I will bring the others back here to see you," Clea says.

"No." I slam my fist on the table. "I don't need them."

"We all need someone, child." Clea folds her hands and leans closer to me. "If anyone needs someone, it is you right now."

"I don't need anyone." I stand and move away from the table. "Don't bring them here. I don't want to see them."

Skeele twists in the bench to face me. "You're not thinking straight."

"What do you know?" I snap. "You just partook in the greatest mindfuck of my life. How could I think straight?"

I walk to the gate and tell the Deacon that I want to go back to my room. He takes me without question, leaving Skeele and Clea to continue their discussion.

I flop down on the bed and press my hands over my eyes. This is all turning to shit. I'm trying to keep them safe by not involving them, that's why I went to the Earthen plane. Now Clea is going to bring them here. This is exactly what I don't want. I don't want my friends to see me like this; weak, emotional, restrained against my will. It's been a long time since I was like this. Not since Jim. Not since that first group of Hellions that nearly killed me.

Noah has a giant grin plastered on his face. I knew I shouldn't have come to see them. I should've stayed in my cell and ignored my Deacon when he came to collect me for visitation.

"Where's Thrush?" I ask, worried.

"Jed and Shay are watching him," Noah says. "Never thought I'd get to see you in lockup. Jailbait all your life and now is when you get put in the slammer."

I roll my eyes. "We could easily change places."

"I'm not so sure about that," Noah winks and scrubs his hair. "I'm too pretty for this place. You know what they say."

"This isn't like the Earthen plane prison," I say, crossing my arms and leaning on the table.

"Are you well?" Nightingale asks.

"I'm fine." I glance to the door, expecting a Deacon to bring Skeele out. My right hand moves to my pocket and slowly shakes the cement and dirt out.

"We are going to get you out," Noah says.

———

The Hellions visit the next week.

Klaus, Chel, and Tukka look out of place in the visitation room. They take up so much space I pause at the door, afraid to enter. It seems like there isn't enough air in the room to breathe with them all there.

Klaus smiles. "There she is." He pats his pockets. "I brought you something." He pulls out four vials of blood.

"You can bring that in here?" I ask.

"They didn't search us," Chel says, leaning into the sliver of a shadow against the wall.

"Have you gotten in any fights yet?" Tukka asks, baring his own fangs. "I've got a bet going."

"Kinda hard when I'm locked up in solitary."

Klaus wrinkles his forehead. "For this long?"

I nod.

"Where's Skeele?" he asks.

"Down the hall from me but I haven't seen him much. They keep him away. Don't let us talk." I sigh. "Not that I want to talk to that liar."

Chel makes a face, and his eyes linger to where my hand is tucked into my pocket, scraping out dirt.

"We'll storm the Safe House," Klaus suggests. "We'll get you out. They can't do this in your own realm."

"I should be out soon," I promise. "Hey, have you ever seen any birds in the ground around here?"

The Hellions think for a moment before Chel says, "There are ground owls." He points to the edge of the Safe House. "The land is cleared, mostly dirt over there. I saw their burrows on the way in." His eyes roam to the pile of dirt that's under my seat. "What are you doing?"

"Don't speak of it," I warn. "Did you all know Skeele went to find me on the Earthen plane?"

All three Hellions close their mouths and look at each other. I guess they weren't preparing themselves for my question.

"You're a bunch of asshats," I say. "I didn't need him."

"He couldn't serve the throne without you in Hell," Klaus says. "It is our duty."

"Would someone have followed Lucifer?" I ask.

"You should talk to Skeele about it," Tukka says. "Don't bite his head off."

"Too late," I warn. "I brought it up when I noticed his matching scars." I hold up my arm with the fern-like pattern from the lightning strike. "That was a few weeks ago."

"Cool," Klaus says, stepping closer to get a better look. "Is that from lightning?"

"Yes." I rub my arm, remembering the tingle.

"You match." Klaus makes a face of satisfaction. "That's a sign."

"Of what?" I shake the rest of the dirt out of my pocket and brush my dusty hands off on my pants.

"A sign of something important." Klaus looks entirely too excited over the prospect that Skeele and me were struck by lightning at the same time.

"Deacons told me we were tossed out of the Earthen plane. That's all. Nothing special but battle scars," I say.

Klaus strokes his beard and narrows his eyes on my arm. "Sure."

———

Jed and Shay visit. I contemplate hiding in my room, but I owe these two. Of all my visitors, I *have* to attend this visitation. I owe them too much to blow them off.

"Hey," Shay leans forward and moves to grip my fist. Her hand hovers over mine.

"It's okay," I lift my fist and let her touch me. "I'm glad to see you. Are you both doing okay?"

"No complaints from this department," Jed says, inspecting me. His fingers tap on the wooden table between us in a rapid beat.

"Are you nervous?" I ask.

He tips his head toward the Deacon. "You think they know what I am?"

"I'm sure. They tend to know everything. Or at least they think they do." I make quick action of emptying my pocket.

A few moments later, Skeele walks in the room. Jed stands and claps him on the shoulder. "Hey man, you alright in there?"

Skeele says, "As well as I can be."

There's a moment of awkwardness. Jed wants to ask Skeele something but as he casts hesitant glances in my direction, I get the sense he doesn't want me to hear.

"I already know," I finally say. "I know he glamoured himself and followed me."

"Hey, man, it worked." Jed smiles and slaps Skeele on the shoulder again. "You brought her back."

Skeele winces and holds up a hand. "Easy." He rolls his shoulders. "My assigned method of contrition has been physical."

"They couldn't give you some prayers to say?" Jed asks, lifting his hand and inspecting Skeele's back. "Dicks."

"I go back next week and they tell me if I'm forgiven." Skeele rubs his hands together and refuses to look in my direction. "My father was a Hellion. I've had worse."

"We have got to get you all out of there," Shay says, patting my hand.

"I have a plan–" I start to say.

"It will not work," Skeele argues.

"I've dug a hole. It's almost completed." I lower my voice. "I should be done by next week."

"Good," Skeele says. "At least you can get out of here."

"Wait, wait." Jed holds up his hands. "We can't leave Skeele in here." He presses fingertips to his head for a moment. "Tell me more."

"The hole is small," I say. "I can get out. He won't fit."

Shay turns to face Jed. "She can get out. I can go in. Then you all can storm the place and get out Skeele." She leaves her hand on mine. "Can you still poof from place to place?"

"Not since I was struck by lightning." I shake my head.

"Jed could do a glamour. We've been practicing." She touches Jed's arm. "Show her. She should know."

Jed's fingers dance in rhythmic spellcasting and Shay turns into a mirror image of me.

"Holy shit." I lean forward and touch her hair. "That's amazing."

"Jed's been practicing new spells from his book," Shay says.

"Have you been pretending to be me?" I ask.

"We had to," Jed says. "The Deacons showed up and the new Hellions were spreading rumors. She didn't do anything you wouldn't do." A mischievous smile lifts the corners of his mouth. "So next week. You get out. Shay can get in. Skeele, create a distraction. Maybe start a fight. Then we raid. Watch this." Jed's fingers move again, and he disappears then reappears a few minutes later. "We can get in, get the keys, get Skeele and Shay and get out. You know the layout. You can lead us while we are cloaked."

The plan sounds good. I think it could work. "Is there a backup plan?" I ask.

"I just thought of this like two minutes ago. I haven't thought of a backup plan," Jed says.

I nod. "Let's do it."

———

The next week, my tunnel is completed. The only problem is I'll have to displace the little burrowing owls while I crawl through.

During the day the Hellions visit, and we solidify the plan. The Deacons don't have security like a normal prison since this is more of a spiritual setting. Churches don't have security, neither do the Deacons.

After dinner, I crawl through the tunnel. My heart is steadily beating faster and faster as I follow the dim light in the distance. When I come to the little burrowing owls, I set them on my shoulder and take them along for the ride. When I finally get to the opening, I pause to take in my surroundings. The tunnel isn't far from the Safe House wall. The opening is in a dip in the land that looks like a retention pond. I scoot out, dirt covering my white scrubs and falling out of my hair.

I see motion in the tree line. The Hellions are there. So is Jed and Shay. She looks just like me. I scramble toward them. When I reach the shadows, Klaus grabs me and pulls me in for a tight hug. I let him hold on to me until he's ready to release me.

Noah and Nightingale aren't here. I wouldn't expect it. They have to watch Thrush. We have enough people.

"Ready?" I ask Shay.

She nods and walks away. I grab her arm to stop her. "Just wait for us. We'll get you out."

Shay pats my hand. "I know, Meg. I know you'll get me out."

The little owls hop around the entrance to the tunnel as Shay climbs inside.

"How long should we give her?" Jed asks.

"A few minutes, then we follow the next Deacon inside."

Jed casts his spells and we are all invisible, then we make our way to the front door.

———

Skeele

Skeele waited, pacing his cell, knowing what was transpiring down the hall. Meg was switching places with Shay, and then they'd be freed. Hopefully. It all sounded too easy. But Skeele no longer cared. If Meg was free, that's all he could ask for. She didn't belong in this Safe House prison. The Deacons had tormented them for long enough.

A metal door squealed. Shit. Skeele pressed his face to the bars hoping Meg and Shay had switched places in time. Footsteps echoed. Many footsteps.

A handful of Deacons stopped in front of Skeele's door. "Let's go." They readied their batons as one opened the door.

Skeele held up his hands in defeat. He just wanted to see if Shay was there.

"Kinda late for interrogation," Skeele said.

"Move," a Deacon ordered.

Skeele behaved. He left the cell without fighting and walked down the hall. His stomach sank when he saw Meg's cell door was also open and no one was inside.

Shit.

A Deacon shoves Skeele from behind. "Move."

They led him to the interrogation room.

Meg was there.

Skeele blinked. Meg didn't make it out. She turned to look at him, a hopeful smile spread across her face. Skeele nodded as he realized this wasn't Meg.

Meg would have greeted him with less excitement. It had been less and less since she found out he was Kal and he'd lied to her. She hadn't smiled in all the weeks they'd been imprisoned.

The man at the center of the desk-of-questioning tapped his gavel. "You're both here for some clarification. You're keeping secrets from each other."

Skeele and Shay looked at each other.

The door creaked and Skeele felt familiar energy enter the room. He sniffed the air and recognized the real Meg and the other Hellions.

"Skeele," the man on the left said. "You ate a family of Newcomers. This is forbidden."

"I was hungry." Skeele replied.

"An entire family, before they had time to reach us." The man at the desk was disgusted. "There are few rules in Hell. Surely you can follow the simplest one."

"It was an emergency." Skeele rolled his shoulders, wishing the others would hurry and get them out.

"What kind of an emergency?"

"Meg was dying," Skeele said.

"You killed to save the ruler of Hell?"

"Yes." Skeele cleared his throat. "And I'd do it again. I was born and bred to serve the throne."

One man tapped his fingers together. "You are like your father, so faithful to Hell."

"There is no other way to be." Skeele lifted his chin. Proud. He was a Hellion. Different than the previous ones, but a Hellion none the less. He'd studied and read and trained. And Sparrow had taught him to be better just before turning into a monster himself.

There is a long pause before the men turned their attention on Shay.

"We need to discuss your situation," the man to the left said.

Shay pressed her lips together.

"The Queen of Hell should not be trying to abort her fetus or be acting recklessly. You were doing drugs to harm your unborn child. God cast you out of the Earthen plane with force. What do you have to say?" the man said.

A feeling of dread combined with the need to be sick flooded Skeele.

Meg was pregnant.

Meg was pregnant. All the vomiting and strange behavior was making sense. He wanted to slap himself. He should've known better. He should've done something. He could have helped her if he'd known.

The fake Meg never said a thing, but in the back of the room Skeele heard Meg's voice quietly say, "Break the glamour. This is not her sin to answer for."

MEG

Shame.

That's the only feeling I have. Complete and utter shame. It's bone deep. Tattooed on my soul. I have never felt more shame in my life.

Everyone in the room heard. I can't let Shay answer to my sins. Those are mine, not hers. And they are no longer secret.

Skeele's jaw is slack, like he can't believe it. I can't look at him. I keep my eyes on the men at the center of the desk of questioning and cross the room to stand next to Shay. Her glamour fades and blue hair returns.

Now I have a giant pile of shit to dig myself out of.

Dig Deep Down

I can kill them all and go on with my life. I can drain them dry. Every one. The Hellions, the Deacons, Skeele, Jed, and Shay. No one will know. No one but me. I can think up some lies to tell the others. It's not like I haven't killed to survive before. This would be... this would be... nothing.

A giant lump forms in my throat. My head hurts. My heart hurts. I can't kill them. I have to protect them. That's what I was trying to do by running away but the Deacons and God destroyed that plan for me. Dicks.

"What do you want from me?" I ask, walking to the front of the room to stand in front of Shay and protect her.

The men at the desk-of-questioning whisper to each other for a few moments before one raises his hand. "We propose a trial since you aren't telling us the truth."

I open my mouth to speak.

Brows rise, putting me in my place.

My mouth snaps shut.

"You sit on trial, Meg. And a jury will decide your fate.

Not us. Deacons keep the balance." The man clears his throat.

"A jury of who?" I ask. "A jury of Deacons. I don't think so." I feel the rage gathering in the center of my chest.

"A jury of your peers. Your friends," the man says.

"I don't want to bring them into this mess. This is my mess, not theirs," I say.

The man at the center of the desk-of-questioning wrinkles his placid face. "The blood of the covenant is thicker than the water of the womb."

I control my blood rage. I don't kill everyone in the room. I suck it up and watch the Deacons as they bring in desks and chairs and set up the room like a courtroom.

It's been a long time since I was in a real courtroom. The last time was when me and Noah stole that car as teenagers and spent the weekend in juvie. This feels much different. I suppose because I'm an adult now and I've done a few things that are a lot worse than stealing a car and going for some joyrides on a Friday night.

Omens Between
the Veil

A gavel falls. I sit and look to my left. The Deacon who brought me back and forth from my cell is sitting there. It's all very dream-like.

The door opens and another Deacon ushers a line of people into the room and toward the jury seats.

Noah, Nightingale, Shay, Jed, Klaus, Tukka, Chel, Klaus, Teari, Gabriel, and Skeele; they are all sitting to the right of me, looking utterly surprised.

Deacon leans close to whisper to me. "I think we have enough evidence."

"For what? To lock me up for a lifetime in this place? I'll be here until the end of days."

He tries to pat my hand, but I jerk it away.

My Deacon stands and addresses the men from the desk-of-questioning. "I'd like to call our first witness, Nightingale."

Nightingale makes her way to the witness stand.

"How did you meet Meg?" Deacon asks, barely giving her time to sit.

"We met in the basement of my family home."

"Why were you in the basement?"

"That's where my father locked us up." Nightingale's face is placed, serious as shit.

"Can you talk more about that?"

"I was crazy. My family was cursed. Me and Sparrow got the worst of it. Remiel, my father, was embarrassed. He didn't want Meg with Sparrow and he didn't want anyone to see me. So, he locked us in the basement."

"How did Meg react to being locked up with you?"

"She told my father he was a dick then she stole Sparrow away in the night."

"And you eventually went with Meg also?" Deacon asks.

"Yup."

Deacon crosses his arms and taps his chin, narrowing his eyes on Nightingale. "Do you think Meg deserves your friendship? Or, even more, your alliance?"

"She deserves it more than she knows." Nightingale goes into stories of our adventures together. Her marriage, her birth, her death. "Meg saved my baby during the fast-Zombie War. She didn't have to take Thrush and hide him. She could have left him to the will of the Archangels. Meg is more than a friend. She's family. It might be hard for her to comprehend that feeling because she's never had any before. But I don't hold that against her because she never held my being batshit-crazy against me."

Nightingale whistles a light melodic trill that brings a tear to my eye.

———

"How did you meet Meg?" Deacon asks Noah.

"We went to school together. Same hometown."

"You've known her for years?"

"Most of our lives."

"But then you died."

Noah raises his hands in defeat. "Sure did. Dead as a doornail."

"Who found you in Hell?"

Noah points. "Meg did."

"I will not ask about this rap-sheet." Deacon waves a handful of papers. "Tell me, why did you friend Meg in childhood?"

"Because she was hot." He quips but then his smile fades, and he clears his throat. "Because she needed a friend. I used to bring her lunch. Her dad never fed her, she was tiny. So skinny. I watched her pick through the garbage after lunch. She would hide from the lunch ladies who tried to give her the leftovers from the lunch line. She was too proud for that."

Deacon nods and paces. "It seems you know a side of Meg that none of us have seen."

"Probably."

"Did you have a romantic relationship with her?"

"For a little bit but we were better as friends."

"I'd like to try something if you'd allow it." Deacon holds up a glass ball that's appeared out of thin air. "These are your memories. I'd like to play your memories of Meg throughout childhood."

"Sure." Noah agrees.

Deacon holds up the ball, and light from the window

passes through. Above, memories play like a movie in the clouds.

They see it all. Things I'd forgotten, things I never wanted to remember. Noah watching me fight a dog on a chain for that peanut butter sandwich, digging in the trash for clothes, the towel full of holes, the dirty mattress on the floor of my filthy childhood bedroom.

When it finally stops, Deacon says, "Thank you, Noah. You are free to go back to your seat."

I feel a little bit like crying and a little bit like punching someone. I never wanted everyone to see all that shit. They didn't need to know John Lewis raised me like a dog in the backyard.

———

"How do you know Meg?" the Deacon asks Jed.

"I first met her in my shop. She came to me for a tattoo." He holds up his arms, showing off his ink.

"Did she know what you were?"

"She didn't know. I had to explain myself."

"You were comfortable explaining yourself to her? You've been in hiding for so long."

"She was in hiding at the time too. We were kindred. Plus, she needed a tattoo, and she could see my blue light." Jed wags a finger. "Only the safe ones can see blue."

"Any problems after meeting Meg?"

Jed rubs his neck. "She did bite me once." He laughs lightly. "It didn't hurt. It was kinda nice, kinda sexy." He clears his throat and sits up straight. "But then she ran off with Sparrow. Our paths crossed again when the zombies started taking over on the Earthen plane."

"And she brought you to Hell against your will?"

"Nope." Jed shakes his head with certainty. "Never against my will. She's never forced me to do anything." He pauses. "Well, besides tattooing Gabriel but that situation wasn't terrible."

———

Shay takes the stand and Deacon begins his questioning.

"Was that the first time you met Meg?"

"Yes, she rescued us from a house that was under siege with the dead. Jed and I were going to die. Then she showed up at the window and did that *poof* thing. And got us out of there."

"You're full human?" Deacon asks.

"Yes."

"How do you feel about being in Hell? You don't necessarily belong here."

"I hope to stay here." Shay tilts her head like no one is going to tell her what to do with her life. "I spent plenty of time on the Earthen plane and Hell has been much nicer to me. I have freedom and safety here. I have people like I've never had before."

"Does Meg ever scare you?"

"Of course. I can tell she's struggling. But most of us are. I can't imagine the things she feels responsible for. But I can tell you when Nightingale and Sparrow were injured, she did *everything* in her power to get them to safety. And when Thrush was stolen by Demore, she never slept until he was home. Most humans care less about their own children than Meg cared for Thrush. Do you know how many missing children there are on the Earthen plane? How many kids are abused, stolen, left to raise themselves and given nothing?" Shay is shaking. She tucks a piece of blue hair behind her ear. "Meg isn't perfect. Neither am I. But Meg tries, even if she doesn't realize it."

———

Tukka looks uncomfortable in the hot seat. The Deacon asks questions about being a Hellion under my rule. Tukka's answers are neutral and straightforward.

"Did you ever see Meg hurt someone?"

Tukka glances at Skeele. "Hurt them how?"

"With her teeth. Her power." Deacon replies.

"It was always in self-defense." Tukka rubs his dark-red cheek. "Once I tried to train her how to fight. I was generous in my mocking."

"How does she fight?"

"Fair enough. Better when she's fed on fresh blood."

"Explain."

"She cut my leg and nearly ate me for dinner."

"How did you get out of that situation?"

Tukka chuckles. "I flew away."

Ouch. That burns.

Klaus and Chel each have a turn on the stand. They discuss our hunt for the basilisk.

"What did Lucifer do with the basilisk babies after he caught a mother?" Deacon asks.

Both Hellions looked uncomfortable when they replied. "Grilled them for dinner."

"What did Meg do with the basilisk babies?"

"Put them in a tank and took care of them."

I shiver recalling their slimy lips sucking the poison out of my arm. I never thought to eat them. That just seems kinda wrong.

———

"I met Meg in Hell the first time," Teari says. "It was a rescue mission."

"Were you successful?" Deacon asks.

"Always." Can't beat Teari's confidence.

"You're close to Meg?"

"As close as she'll let me get. She has walls up."

"Tell me about the Zombie War on the Earthen plane." Deacon paces in front of our desk.

"I went to find Sparrow and Meg. No one had heard from them for a long time."

"How did you find Meg?"

"God led me to her. There were signs."

"You found Meg, then Sparrow, then you were bitten by the dead?"

Teari holds up her healed hands. "Chopped off both my arms. Meg helped."

My cheeks flame. It was not my proudest moment.

"She cut off your arms?" Deacon asks.

Teari makes a flippant motion. "I made her."

"And then she abandoned you on the Earthen plane?"

"She came back for me."

"And then she locked you up in the burning caves?"

"I was a danger to myself."

"What happened next?"

"She came back with a vial of my father's blood and healed me."

"I thought you were the healer?" Deacon asks. "You *are* the personal healer to King Gabriel."

"All of that is true. But Meg healed me. She saved me."

The Deacon nods as he moves closer and sets his hand on the box of the witness stand. "Strange how she keeps saving people. But she fights so hard against saving herself."

Ouch. What in the absolute hell is wrong with this guy? I slam my fist on the desk and stand. "Objection!"

The men from the desk-of-questioning focus on me.

"I want that comment scratched from the record," I say.

Deacon chuckles. "Sorry. I was out of line." He sits next to me as Teari moves across the room.

"I thought you were on my side?" I seethe.

"I am." The Deacon smiles. "Just making a point.

––––––

"You are the current Hellion Commander?" Deacon asks Skeele.

"Yes."

"Are you close to your Queen?" Deacon asks.

"As close as one can be."

"Would you say you're bonded to each other?"

"No." Skeele's voice is sharp. "To be bonded both parties would have to be agreeable to that."

"But she takes your blood?"

"Yes."

"You offer yourself to her. You kneel at her side?"

"Always."

"Your relationship should be more."

Skeele stares straight ahead at the wall. "It is what Meg allows. Nothing more."

"Were you aware that Meg was with child?" Deacon asks.

"No." Skeele shakes his head.

"Did she act sick around you? There have been no signs?"

"She vomited. I thought she was disgusted by me."

"Why would you think that?"

"She has said that she hates the Hellions, they disgust her."

Oh Christ, I am the biggest jackass in all of the realms. I want to hide in a hole.

"But you never left her side? You've been loyal all this time?" Deacon asks.

"I vowed to. It is my duty. I was born and bred to be a Hellion. There is nothing else."

"So much so that you tracked her down on the Earthen plane? You tricked her into thinking you were human."

Skeele shrugs, guilty. "It was the only way I could see."

"Actually, the others colluded with you to find her. Isn't that right?"

"Yes."

"Why would you all go after her?"

"She belongs with us. Life isn't the same without her. Hell is not the same without her."

I swallow the lump in my throat. What have I done to this Hellion? How could I never see it before?

"Do you know whose child she is pregnant with?" Deacon asks.

Oh fuck. No. No. No. No. This is not his information to tell. This is my secret to release. This is mine. No one knows but Teari. No one. Panic creeps up my chest, nearly choking me. I feel like a trapped animal in the smallest cage.

"No." Skeele says. "It's none of my business. It is only

my business to serve Meg, to feed her when she allows." His leathery wings shiver and something flickers behind his dark eyes.

I stand, my chair falling over with the force of how quickly I move. "It's yours," I shout across the room to Skeele. "The baby is yours."

He looks shocked, troubled. I don't know how to read him because I've been so selfish. I never took much time to learn about him, I only took from him. I took his blood. I took his sex. And, now I see it, I took his love and stomped all over it. What the fuck is wrong with me?

No apology can make up for this. None.

Skeele's features are stone as he is released from the stand and returns to the jury.

———

"Our next witness, Sparrow," Deacon announces. Oh shit. My body feels like it's on fire with warring emotions of hate and fear. What the fuck is Sparrow doing here? If they listen to him, I'll surely be in the slammer for eternity.

My Deacon refuses to look in my direction. It's better that way. If looks could kill he'd be ended.

The door slams open and Sparrow walks through. I can't take my eyes off him. His energy fills the room. His giant black wings drape on the floor like a king dragging an extravagant robe. This is a very different Sparrow than the one I traipsed across the northeast with. This is not the quirky Sparrow who was obsessed with collecting feathers. No, this Sparrow is power and anger and menace. I always wondered if I'd even like him once he was back to his normal self. It seems the answer is no. I don't like him. But we are close as family now with Nightingale living in Hell with us. So, I guess we can have mutual respect. As long as he doesn't stab me again.

The Raven King moves to the chair at the front of the room. His darkness is far reaching, and I can feel it inching toward me. The air becomes thick and hard to breathe. If this is a parlor trick, I need to learn how to do it. Energy like that could turn the tables in any argument.

"Please, keep yourself contained," my Deacon says. "We know your history with Meg is turbulent. This is a neutral zone."

Sparrow tips his head like a raven on the phone wire watching food in the middle of a busy road. There was a time that his birdlike mannerisms were comforting.

Deacon clears his throat. "Meg has stated on multiple occasions that you are her hallelujah, heroin, and reason to breathe. What changed?"

Sparrow tips his chin down. "It all started to go a little south when my father threatened her and then she killed him."

I could crawl into a hole right now with those green eyes boring into me. His father was an asshole and Sparrow knows it. Locking up Nightingale was a sin if I ever saw one.

I stand and shout. "How about when you stabbed me to death?"

My Deacon pulls on my arm, forcing me to sit and shushing me. "Stop."

I try to stand again, pointing with venom. "He tried to kill me." I pull at the neck of my shirt. "I have the scars to prove it!"

Ireland-grass green eyes singe my soul. "Remember when you stabbed me in the heart and took the last spec of my grace?" His voice is deep, solemn.

"The Scarecrow told me I had to do it. The Deacons hired the Scarecrow to fuck everything up," I say, my hands shaking. "I found you!" I shout. "I found you and saved you and healed you after the fast-Zombie War. We are even."

Sparrow presses his lips in a straight line and he nods, knowing.

The Deacon bends to make eye contact and grips both my shoulders. "Sit. Meg."

I suck in a weary breath and wrap my fingers around the arms of my chair. "You're a bunch of fucks." Air whistles as I breathe heavily through my nose, my mouth set in a grim line to hide sharp teeth that want nothing more than to rip out some necks.

Satisfied with my control, Deacon turns and addresses Sparrow again. I glance toward the men at the desk-of-questioning. They don't seem fazed by my outburst.

The Deacon asks, "You brought something to show the jury?"

Sparrow reaches in his pocket and pulls out the Argentavis feather Clea gave us. He passes it to the Deacon. "What is this?" the Deacon asks.

"An omen." Sparrow motions in my direction. "From her mother."

Deacon holds up the feather into the light passing through the room and the omen play for all to see.

Wars. Blood and death. Good and evil. A dead Sparrow. A motherless child and a fatherless child. Light and dark. The Earthen plane and the Ethereal realms. A burst of light. An explosion. Fear and pain. Emptiness. A dark, never-ending vat of emptiness that would suck every joyful moment right out of me.

I remember that moment I shuddered in his arms, soaking wet. *"Just remember, we are invincible together."* I thought he was the one person who has ever shown me love and caring and truth.

"Your interpretation of the omen?" the Deacon asks, knocking his knuckles on the table in front of me. Somehow, he knew I was getting lost in my head.

"It all happened," Sparrow says matter-of-factly. "Just like Clea prophesized. Just not like we thought it would."

"Hm." Deacon rubs his chin. "Prophecy can be like that. Gray and malleable. None of us really know with absolute certainty what will happen. What did you think would happen?"

"That she was mine."

The way Sparrow says it sends a shiver up the back of my neck.

"But she isn't." Sparrow leans to the side and sets his elbow on the arm of the chair. "Especially now that she is with child. My Kingdom will yield in our desire for revenge. The Archangels yield as well. As long as my sister resides in Meg's realm, we will truce."

Sparrow tips his chin and whistles a light trill in Nightingale's direction.

———

"Our next witness is going to be delayed," my Deacon says. "He has a long way to travel."

A gavel falls with a loud thud.

"We'll break for lunch." The man in the middle stands.

Deacon escorts me to my cell in solitary. I'm surprised they didn't search it after I switched places with Shay.

"You want something to eat?" Deacon asks. "I can have a tray delivered."

My stomach lurches at the thought of food but I'm

hungry. "I want an orange soda and chicken fried steak and a side of curly fries with cheese dipping sauce."

"I'll see what I can do." Deacon walks away. "Don't get too nervous. Maybe take a nap."

Yeah right. Take a nap in the middle of this.

Deacon's footsteps echo as he walks away. Metal squeals as they slide the doors closed and lock me inside, twice.

I move the bed and find the tunnel is still there. They didn't fill it or put me in another cell. I sit, cross-legged. This is too easy. All I have to do is crawl through again and escape to freedom. I can be done with this crock of shit and move on. Running away would be better than killing everyone in the room. It would be better than eternity in this cell.

I tip my head and hear the gentle cooing of the burrowing owls. In the tunnel's darkness, the light from my cell reflects on their eyes. They walk closer, old friends in dark places. There isn't enough room for both of us in that tunnel. I'd have to push them out.

I can't crawl through that tunnel because I will never be free without my friends.

What would Andy Dufresne do? I move to the bed and sit, waiting for my food with my back against the wall. I could do well to believe in the power of hope. That's all we really have, after all.

Tip the Scales of
Darkness

The person sitting on the witness stand doesn't look like a person at all. It is an opaque cloud that's struggling to take shape. It swells and ripples, the edges lighten to mist.

"Can you hear me?" my Deacon asks the cloud.

"Yes," the cloud replies with a voice too familiar to forget.

It's Jack!

I turn to look at Noah and Nightingale. They are both leaning forward in their seats. Noah rubs his mouth.

"Thank you." Deacon stands. "I'd like to present Jack Cooper, brother to Noah Cooper, husband to Nightingale, childhood friend of Meg."

I never thought I'd hear Jack's voice again. I can't stop looking at the cloud, trying to will it to take form so I remember him as more than a teether for the undead during the fast-Zombie War. I'd give a lot to see him whole and not covered in blood and bite marks.

"You met Meg in childhood?" Deacon asks.

"Yes," the cloud with Jack's voice replies.

"Then you died and went to Hell. Is that correct?"

"Sure is."

"Who helped you find your way to a Safe House to repent and find your place in the afterlife?"

"Meg."

"Was she alone?"

"No. She was with a Scarecrow. I guess she'd gotten in some trouble."

"You'd gotten in some trouble too. You committed the worst crime of humankind, correct?"

"I killed John Lewis, but it was well deserved." There is no remorse in Jack's voice.

"What would make you do such a thing? Commit your soul to Lucifer for a lower demon?"

"He hurt Meg. She didn't deserve it."

"So, you killed in defense of your friend?"

"I'd do it again. One million times over again. I'd end him for what he did to her." Jack's voice is dead-cold.

Deacon clears his throat. "She brought you to a Safe House but you didn't stay."

"I was worth 400 souls. You all were using me as leverage to pay for Remiel's death. If you ask me, he deserved it. I would have never survived repenting. I would have wasted away to nothing in the Safe House. You all knew it. The whole situation was a load of horse shit. You tried to play me."

"You went to Heaven though," Deacon clarifies.

"I did. I made a deal for the people I love."

"And you were a King." Deacon's voice has a hopeful lilt.

"Until the fast-Zombie War broke through our ceiling." The cloud ripples and heaves and swirls like a tornado. "Now I am nothing."

Nightingale makes a noise from the jury area. Noah wraps an arm around her shoulder and tucks her against him. I remember the chaos in which they died every time I look at Nightingale's scars on her face.

"I am sorry the tragedy occurred." Deacon looks solemn. "I have one last question." He inches closer to the cloud swirling. "In your opinion, does Meg deserve friends like you who would kill for her?"

"Of course."

"Why is that?"

"Because she'd do the same for one of us."

He's not wrong. I cross my arms over my chest feeling cold and empty from hearing Jack's voice.

The cloud slowly dissipates. Without a goodbye, Jack leaves us again.

———

Gabriel is last. He answers the Deacon's questions about our history together and the battles we've faced. He tells them about losing me. About Sparrow being assigned to watch me, losing me, then the curse taking over. Gabriel tells them about the fast-Zombie War and the safety I offered him when the Archangels turned against him.

"I would give anything to change the way things went with Meg," Gabriel says, "but we thought we were protecting her. If I can do better by my grandchild, I promise I'll do everything I can."

Gabriel's eyes bore into mine and I want to turn away as my cheeks flush with embarrassment. This is not John Lewis who hit me and kicked me and starved me as a child. This is not the lower Demon who raised me under a roof of abuse and hate. John Lewis would have kicked me to the curb if he'd found out I was pregnant. Not Gabriel.

"Could you tell me for the record, how many heartbeats do you hear from Meg's body? There's no room for error."

Gabriel holds up his fingers like a peace sign. "Two." His voice cracks and a single tear drips down his cheek to get lost in his white beard.

I have never known Gabriel to be so emotional, but there is something about this moment; the confession, the truth that's brought tears to his eyes. I've never seen Gabriel in this state before.

———

There are no more witnesses called to the stand. Instead, the men at the desk-of-questioning release the jury to discuss my fate.

My Deacon sits thin-lipped and offers nothing to me in terms of what to expect. My stomach growls loudly and I'm sure everyone in the room hears it. I sink down in my chair wishing I could dig a hole and hide forever inside of it.

When the door finally opens again, everyone files in and sits, except for Nightingale.

Nightingale stands and clears her throat. "One who is never given love, does not know how to give love or receive it." Her hands are clasped across her middle and she is very still before she says, "We the jury have determined that the only way to decide Meg's fate is to weigh her heart against the feather of truth." Nightingale sits and waits.

The men at the desk nod their heads in agreement.

"What does that mean?" I ask my Deacon.

"An old law, not used for many millennia," he replies.

The feather of truth is white with brown stripes. It's

brought into the room on an embellished glass platter along with a gold scale.

"Your heart," the man at the center of the desk-of-questioning says, expectantly.

Gruesome images fill my mind of someone ripping open my chest and taking my heart out.

"Go get your jar of feathers," my Deacon says.

I stare at him. My jar of feathers is on my nightstand.

"Go get it." He motions with his hand. "Poof."

I close my eyes since this hasn't worked in a while and I don't trust myself.

Poof.

I'm standing in my bedroom in the castle. Elise's feathers are where they've been for a while now. My heart. I walk forward, pick up the jar, and tip it to the side.

I could go. I could run. I could *poof* to anywhere. I could *poof* to the moon or the bottom of the ocean and they wouldn't be able to find me. "What should I do?" I ask the feathers.

The urge to return and face my fate is strong. Maybe this is what I deserve: a fresh start. Maybe I can finally accept what I've become. Maybe I can finally accept what grows in my belly. I settle my hand over my womb. I never thought I'd get another chance. I never thought I deserved another chance. I've never embraced my place in this existence or my throne or the people who surround me. I have hope that maybe, just maybe, I'm deserving of it all. I must face the music.

Poof.

I set the jar of feathers on the desk.

"Just one," my Deacon says. "And we're glad you came back."

I smile but just a tiny bit. I choke down the emotion

filling my chest and the tears forming in the corner of my eyes. I open the jar and take out a feather. At the desk, one of the old men has moved the golden scale and set the feather of destiny in its place. He motions for me to add mine.

My heart beats in my ears as I take the single feather from the jar and walk to the front of the room. I set it on the open tray of the scale and hold my breath as the scale tilts from side to side.

"If your heart is heavy, you go elsewhere." The man at the center of the desk says.

I swallow the lump in my throat as the tilting of the scale slows. My feather, my heart, it tips up and down and I can't get an idea of where it will stop.

Finally, it slows. It sits even with the feather of destiny, then raises.

"What does that mean?" I ask the men at the desk.

"Your heart is true. You will make the right decisions." The gavel falls, hard and heavy and loud. "You are released," the man in the middle of the desk says.

"What about Skeele?"

"He can go. His contrition is enough."

I rub my eyes, afraid to turn around and face my friends who have become my family.

"One last thing." My Deacon motions for me to wait. "Your belongings." He passes me the bag I was carrying the day I was struck by lightning. He holds up my old I.D., inspecting. "You're going to need to replace this."

"I know. It doesn't really look like me anymore and I don't live in NY."

"No." The Deacon rubs his fingers over the card like he's polishing a fork. "This one will just get you entry into

Canada." He hands it back to me. "This is more official for your current situation."

The license is covered in strange markings, something like the runes Jed uses, and my picture is replaced with one more up to date.

Who Says You Can't
go Home

We leave the Safe House together. The Hellions branch out and surround us, watching for danger on the crumbling road.

The surroundings look familiar. "Is this the Safe House in Auburn?"

"Yes," Klaus says.

"It's a distance from the castle," I say.

"We can get everyone back if we fly," Klaus says.

"I still can't fly," I say.

"Jed and Shay have to be carried. So would you." Klaus rubs his hands on his pants.

I say goodbye to Gabriel and Teari.

"That arm," Teari warns. "Get the basilisk on it. Then come see me."

"Sure," I promise.

Gabriel hugs me tightly and whispers in my ear. "Whoosh-whoosh-whoosh, that's what it sounds like. Faster than your heartbeat."

He takes Teari's hand and *poof*, they go back to his kingdom.

Nightingale fades to nothing waving to me as she travels back to Thrush.

Noah approaches me. "Why did you break the tether?" he asks.

"I wanted you to be with your family. I wanted you to have time with them and to keep Thrush safe. You didn't need to run all over creation just to find me sodas and Twinkies and waffles with fried chicken."

"Maybe I enjoyed it." He touches my hand. "I meant what I said on the stand. Put the tether back."

Noah has always been the best friend a girl could have, and I ache for every moment of laughter we've ever had to come back into our lives. I want to throw bird seed and talk in whistles and chirps and call each other ridiculous names. I've missed it all these months.

"Do it, Meg," he urges.

I nod and replace the tether to our souls.

"Now," Noah gives me a dashing smile, "What do you want to eat? I'll have it waiting in your room."

I opt for waffles and fried chicken with chocolate milk. "Enough for two," I say. "Please."

"Shit," Noah chuckles. "Manners and everything."

"What can I say? I'm turning a new leaf."

"Let's hope." Noah disappears.

Chel approaches Shay and offers to fly her back to the castle. Shay glances to Jed and he nods, pointing to Tukka. "You take me," he says.

The four of them take to the air.

I'm left alone with Skeele and Klaus.

They're giving me an option. It's easy to see. I get an option after all those times I shafted Skeele and chose Gabriel or the Argentavis or traveled on my own.

Do better, Meg. I tell myself.

I've been with Skeele and embraced it before. My time with Kal was great. No judgement, no horns or blood. It was Skeele all along. I don't have to push him away. I accepted his invitations to dates and other things. If this is going to work, I can't keep pushing him away.

"Will you take me back?" I ask Skeele.

He nods, solemn. And I get the feeling he's guarded and just following orders. He's probably used to doing that. Not getting attached just like I said. He was definitely attached as Kal and I get the feeling he's attached as Skeele; he's just great at hiding it.

Klaus launches himself into the air and flies away.

I'm finally alone with Skeele.

"I'm sorry," I say.

"You don't–"

I press my fingers against his heart. "I do. I was afraid. I was wrong." I slide my hands up his chest and round his neck.

"Don't be afraid. I'm here." Skeele steps closer, closing the distance between us until our bodies are flush.

"I told you not to get attached." My eyes burn.

"It was too late." Skeele wraps his arms round my shoulders and holds me close. He lifts me into his arms, takes a step, and launches us into the air. His leathery wings beat hard and strong as he flies us through Hellsky.

I close my eyes and raise my face to the ochre sun. I should have let him carry me all those other times, because this feels right and safe.

———

"Child," Clea calls as I enter the giant door of the burning caves. "You're back."

Her cool, Astral form hugs me.

"They didn't ask you to speak at the trial," I say.

Red lips stretch to a smile. "Can't put a mother on the witness stand for her child. We'd say whatever we needed to. It wouldn't be right."

"Are you saying you'd lie for me?" I ask.

Her image wavers. "There are things I'd do, and the Deacons knew better than to invite me." She walks toward the ballroom and motions for us to follow. "While you were gone, I had planning to do."

Creatures scurry in the shadows as we walk, our shoes echoing on the stone floor. Skeele's footsteps are not far behind mine.

Clea pushes open the ballroom doors and everyone is there.

"Congratulations on your parole!" Noah shouts.

There's a table laden with food. Pizza and slushies, cake and fried chicken, fondu and shrimp cocktail and deviled eggs. Nightingale is skating in circles while Thrush laughs in her arms. She stops near a record player to drop the arm down. *Wake me up Before You Go-Go* starts playing.

Skeele touches my shoulder.

"When I was little, I would sing 'wake me up before the cocoa,'" I say. "Not to anyone, just to myself. In my room. Alone."

Everyone hugs me. And I let them. I squeeze them tight: Chel, Tukka, Klaus, Noah, Jed, Shay, Nightingale, Thrush, and when Gabriel and Teari crash the party a few hours later, I hug them too. There's no Sparrow, or Archangels from the Seven Kingdoms of Heaven. I'm not saying I'd hug them, but right now I wouldn't stab them. Just for tonight, I won't stab them.

As we're eating and dancing, one of the new recruit Hellions enters the Ballroom with a black-dressed Deacon.

I walk over to meet them, Skeele at my shoulder.

"What do you want?" Skeele asks. "We were released, fair and square."

"You were." It's my Deacon, the one who sat next to me during the trial. "But you left this behind."

He holds up the jar of feathers and passes it to me.

I reach for the jar. "Thanks," I say.

My memories of Elise. I rotate the jar and watch the feathers float. When I look up again the Deacon is gone. I wasn't planning on inviting him to stay but a goodbye would have been nice.

"Are you okay?" Skeele asks, watching me warily.

"Yeah." I set the jar on the table with our food and plates.

"It won't be like last time," Skeele says, drawing me to the balcony. "I'm here."

I nod and hold back threatening tears.

"Are you hungry?" he asks, glancing to the shadows. "We don't have to leave the party if you are."

"Until the bloodlust hits at least," I remind him.

He tucks his wings tight against his back. I touch the fern-like scars on his arm.

"So, Kal, did you enjoy being a human?" I ask.

He rubs his neck. "It was an experience. I didn't like not being able to fly." His eyes focus on me. "I didn't like you not taking care of yourself." He touches the matching scars on my arm. "Did this hurt?"

I shake my head. "I don't remember."

He turns me and presses his fingers against two bony ridges on my back. "Did this hurt?"

"What is that?" I ask, trying to get a look over my shoulder.

He smirks, knowing. "Can you feel them?"

"I didn't notice before." It doesn't feel like he's touching my shoulder blades; there's something else there.

Skeele picks me up and launches us into Hellsky.

My stomach churns. "Careful big boy, or you're going to get a faceful of half-digested pizza."

We climb higher into the night sky as he flaps his powerful wings. "None of us came out of the womb with wings. They need an urge to sprout." He searches my face. "Our parents would drop us from the sky. It's the only method we know. Kick the baby bird out of the nest and teach it to fly."

"Don't drop me." I grip around his neck. "I can't." I squeeze my eyes closed. All those times I was flung into the air surge to the forefront of my mind.

"We'll go together. I'd never let you fall. I'd never let you hit the ground. Know that."

I open one eye, afraid.

"Ready?"

I nod. I swallow hard and take a few deep breaths.

Skeele holds me out and stops moving his wings. We drop like a roller-coaster descending that first giant hill. He doesn't let go. He stays. His hands warm under my arms, holding me like no one ever has before.

A warm feeling begins in my chest, radiates across my shoulders and neck, then my back. After it feels like we have been falling for too long, we stop. Gently. Not like that time I fell from the sky and broke every bone in my body.

"Night Owl," Skeele says. "Open your eyes."

I open them, feeling the strange heaviness on my back. Skeele is looking at me like I'm something special. Our feet are on the ground. Skeele releases my elbows.

My wings are dappled gray and white, soft and downy as I run my hands down the sides.

Blinking a few times, my eyes focus slowly and everything changes in the moonlight filtered through Hellsky. My vision is crisp, colors more vibrant, the swishing of the grass audible to my ears like it has never been. There is something more, something beating fast, *lubdub-lubdub-lubdub*. It's faster than most pulses I've heard. Softer too, gentler and pure. The light lilt of a tiny bell.

"Do you hear that?" I ask.

Skeele shakes his head.

I glance down, realizing it's the baby's heartbeat. The one I had tried to silence. The one I'd tried to rid myself of. The one I'd tried to hide and exterminate like it was nothing more than a bug. I am reminded of the day I heard Elise's heartbeat for the first time. I saw her tiny arms and legs moving on the ultrasound in the doctor's office. I loved her in that moment. And not long after she was taken from me.

She was innocent in the war between the Seven Kingdoms of Heaven and Hell and the Earthen plane. She was harmless. But sometimes, men with power must crush innocence to stay relevant.

The sound quickens, *lubdub-lubdub-lubdub*. I can't believe I wanted it gone. I can't believe I would leave it elsewhere. I understand why Gabriel's eyes leaked tears when he said he could hear it. *lubdub-lubdub-lubdub*. It is more, so much more. Hope and inspiration and... home.

EPILOGUE

Teari was right. It was eighteen months. Eighteen months of apologies, forgiveness, and getting my shit straight. I accepted the throne of Hell in all of its glory. I accepted the Hellions as my legion of warriors. We had law and order, and Hell wasn't all that bad for the Demons and the dead. Or at least, that's what they told me. My grandfather led by fear and death for eons. Newcomers rarely found a Safe House during Lucifer's time. Now they are escorted daily and as a result the dead that walk Hell are fewer in numbers. Their souls are not lost. They do not wake up a walking sack of flesh. The Hellions patrol and get them moving in time. The Deacons seem to appreciate the effort. Not once have they interrupted dinner since we left the Safe House the day of my trial-except to return my jar of feathers.

I stopped thinking of Sparrow. I no longer desired revenge for him stabbing me to death that one day. I try to focus on what he taught me-what the entire incident taught me. That it's okay to fall ass over teakettle in love and lust but people change, circumstances change. We can't go back in time and relive those days, but we can build a new home. Something like we've never had before.

Noah and Nightingale raised Thrush in their little corner of Hell. The cemetery has been their paradise. No one bothers them, not even me. Even though I replaced the tether, I do my best to give Noah his freedom and time with Nightingale. Since Jed brought her back, we're not sure how long she'll stay before her soul is whisked away back to death. My hope is she'll be like Clea and Noah, and her Astral form will stay with us forever.

Jed and Shay have stayed at the castle. They tag along with the Hellions, rescuing lost souls and practicing ancient magic. Jed is sure he will come across another Nephilim. But like he's said a thousand times before, they rarely make it past childhood. It doesn't stop him from looking.

We never rebuilt the portals. Each month the Hellions make the rounds to ensure they are nothing but rubble. If someone wants to sneak into Hell, they must use Demore's pond which is heavily warded thanks to Jed.

The basilisk babies grew too big for the castle. We kept two and released the others. One protects Noah and Nightingale's chapel. Two went to Demore's pond. The others went back to the dark waters of the black river in the Adirondacks of Hell.

When the birth finally came, there was no bloodbath like in the books she showed me. There was no gore or torn apart vaginas or vacant eyes. The birth was quiet. The parts of me that hurt during and after, Teari healed almost instantly. Skeele held me and fed me and brushed my hair out of my eyes when Teari set the naked baby on my chest.

"She has dark hair, like you," Skeele said.

I touched his horns and asked, "Not these?"

"No." He shook his head as the baby let out a blat.

"She's mouthy like you too. Looks like she has your temper."

The Hellions made a bassinet out of dark stained wood. In the middle of the night, I sometimes woke to find Skeele rocking it with one foot while he sat reading in the leather club chair.

In the time that followed, I healed. I learned to love. I learned to accept what others gave me. I told Skeele to get attached. I got attached. I grew stronger. I became more than my hunger and bloodlust. Skeele kept my bed warm and my heart full. We had everything I never thought I deserved. For now.

A truce can only last for so long. One day, I know they'll come again. The fast-dead, the Archangels, God. Whoever it may be. Veils of shadows surround us in every realm, filled with secrets and silent wars. A veil of shadows once occluded my vision. It kept me small. It kept me weak. It kept me angry and afraid and filled with venom. It is no more.

-The End-

About the Author

Thank you, thank you, thank you for sticking with the Sparrow Man/Veil of Shadows Series. It took a long time but we finally found an end to Sparrow and Meg's story. I know, it's different than what we wanted. I still love Sparrow. Who couldn't? There's SO much that he and Meg went through. I cried at the ending of Night Owl. I was so sad to see them go. BUT, they are two of my favorite characters and I am hoping to revisit them in the future. They are immortal after all :)

Veil of Shadows is not over. I will continue to write in this world. Up next is Etched in Darkness. Over the next few books we will dive into Jed and Shay's stories. Shay was an unexpected character who showed up in Raven King and she's been tethered in my brain, asking to get out. I'm loving her story of a badass Montana cowgirl who gets caught up in a world of Demons and Angels. You can start their adventure today, there's a preview included at the end of this book!

———

Thank you to my amazing editor, Kristy of EditSchmedit who has stuck with me all of these years and provided plenty of support and edits. One day I'll learn how to use a question mark. It may not be today, it may not be tomorrow, but one day.

M. R. Pritchard writes about the elemental struggle between good and evil, and gods and monsters, and about people who turn into gods and monsters. Usually with a mix of apocalypse or post-apocalyptic setting. She also includes a spec of a love story because what is humanity without love?

M. R. Pritchard is a two-time Kindle Scout winning author, her short story "Glitch" has been featured in the 2017 winter edition of THE FIRST LINE literary journal. Her short story "Moon Lord" has been featured in Chronicle Worlds: Half Way Home (Part of the Future Chronicles) and will be time capsuled on the moon on the Lunar Codex in 2024.

M. R. Pritchard holds degrees in Biochemistry and Nursing. She is a northern New Yorker transplanted to the Gulf Coast of Florida who enjoys coffee, mint chocolate, cloudy days, and reading on the lanai.

Visit her website MRPritchard.com and sign up for her newsletter. You'll get a monthly newsletter with updates, special previews of new projects, and book deals.

If you enjoyed *The Sparrow Man/Veil of Shadows Series*, please leave a review, tell a friend, or gift to a friend. These small acts keep authors writing. Thank you.

Looking for Special Edition Hardcovers? Visit her website for signed and Special Edition versions of stories you love!

ALSO BY M. R. PRITCHARD

<u>Science Fiction/post-apocalyptic:</u>

The Phoenix Project

The Reformation

Revelation

Inception

Origins

Resurrection

The Phoenix Project Compendium Edition

The Safest City on Earth

The Man Who Fell to Earth

Heartbeat

Asteroid Riders Series

Moon Lord

Collector of Space Junk and Rebellious Dreams

<u>Steampunk:</u>

Tick of a Clockwork Heart

<u>Dark Fantasy:</u>

Sparrow Man Series/Veil of Shadows Series

Sparrow Man

Nightingale Girl

Scarecrow

Raven King

Nightjar

Night Owl

Thread the Bone

Fantasy/Fairy Tale Love Story/Romance:

Muse

Forgotten Princess Duology

Midsummer Night's Dream: A Game of Thrones

Poetry/Short Stories

Consequence of Gravity

Preview of Etched in Darkness (unedited)

Running for your life wasn't a sport on the Earthen plane, but for Jed, it was survival. Jed had been on the run since he could walk on two legs and finally escape the creatures that came for him day and night. Since he was Nephilim, this was the way it would always be. He'd been around a while. He'd been hunted for a while. He knew this from the few others he'd met that were like him. They didn't last long, but they traded stories and methods to stay alive. Jed tapped his pocket, feeling the notebook of spells that was left to him by the last Nephilim he'd come across decades ago. Declan wasn't much older that Jed, but he'd lasted by way of spells and runes carved onto every flat surface of his house and belongings. Jed took it one step further and carved those runes into his skin. It was good practice since now he could make a living with the tattoo gun. But, every so often, a creature would walk through the doors of his shop that didn't belong. Like Meg did that one day. Meg with her dark energy and light eyes. There was something about her he didn't understand. She paid in full and held conversation while he tattooed the watercolor sparrow over her heart. He revealed little about himself, it was when she came back again and brought that fallen-Angel Hellion Sparrow that she wound up ruining the pleasant spot he was at in life. Sparrow was all kinds of cursed, Jed could see it the moment he laid eyes on the guy. Worse was that Meg was head over heels in love. He helped them, tattooed them with runes of protection. And all it got him was noticed.

Jed touched the mark on his neck. He also lost a little blood when Meg bit him. Jed tried to shake away the feelings. Lust and heat had filled his body. He remembered touching her waist before he passed out. Whatever she was, he wanted more but he also wanted to never see her again. Meg was trouble. Trouble he didn't have time for if he wanted to stay alive.

Now here he was, on the run again. Making his way away from the crowded cities of the Northeast. Jed headed west, toward the rural towns of the Midwest. With any hope, he'd avoid the dead until someone else took care of them and he'd find a way to avoid Angels and Demons and dead things as well. He'd find food and shelter and hunker down until it was safe again.

Jed stopped under the awning of an empty gas station. The dead hadn't been walking for long, a few months at least, but the destruction and abandon was rapid. Jed glanced through the glass of the gas station and auto shop to see if there was anything inside worth investigating. His pack was heavy with clothes and food, his water jug half-full. He focused on the shelves behind the counter. He could use a smoke. It had been a long time since he set a cancer stick to his lips. He gave up the dirty habit when New York State outlawed them. It surprised him Indiana hadn't outlawed them too.

The sound of shuffling feet broke the afternoon silence. On this daily trek from Walkerton to Kingsbury, Jed hadn't seen much life. He was sure the dead were making their way to nearby Chicago. They always seemed to move with purpose, clustering in small groups. Something drove them.

A man's voice startled Jed. "A large drove of zombies is making their way through California."

Jed walked to the door of the gas station and found the television mounted in the far corner of the waiting area. A map of the U.S. replaces the reporter's image, the movement of the dead is illustrated with green blobs like weather radar. There's a large area of green over southern California, moving north. The area south of the green zone is colored black. A dead zone. Do not go there.

"If you're still in northern California and you're hearing this message, evacuate. Evacuate now! The coast guard has abandoned the west coast. The National Guard has declared California a complete loss."

Jed focused on the spattering of green where he was traveling. The Midwest wasn't overly populated, it would be easier to hunker down. His gaze went to the west coast again. The green blob travelled along a main highway. He found that interesting. The dead didn't care about roads, they moved through forests just as haphazardly as they moved through roads. It was almost like they were following something.

The news reported rubbed his face and looked thoroughly terrified. There were loud thuds from the television, a light fell over and hit the desk where the reporter sat. The reporter stood. "Evacuate now!" he shouted one last time before picking up his chair and throwing it. A dead woman walked across the screen before the screen turned to static.

Jed glanced at the shelves and noticed some of the snack

foods hadn't been completely pillaged. There was a handful of Slim Jims, Oreos, and a few tins of Spam. Jed went for the protein. The sugary cookies might taste good, but he knew he'd be feeling like crap the next day.

He stilled at the shuffling sound again. Turning, he noticed a figure walking down the street.

Jed paused, crouched, and watched the tall man walking down the road. Angel wings were invisible on this plane, but he could see their transparent glimmer. He always knew when they were near, feathered or leathered, he could see the wings in the right light.

This was an Angel. Come to put an end to his life, since he was forbidden and all. They never stopped. Jed traced his footsteps in his mind and tried to think of any clues he could have left behind. He'd been careful on his travels.

Jed whispered a spell of glamour and his fingers tapped in spellcasting. He leaned to the side and didn't see his reflection in the glass window of the gas station. He scooted forward, careful not to step on any debris that would make the Angel walking down the road notice him. He made his way out the door, keeping to the shadows. He stopped once he got around the corner of the building.

The shuffling sound got louder. It didn't seem to bother the Angel walking down the street. He was tall, lithe with muscle, a blade drawn. His clothing was similar to Earthen plane, leathers and linen or jeans and a T-shirt. A Demon he'd be able to spot based on clothing along, they were always in full leather. Dark leather, black or deep red like a kidney bean. The Angel gripped his blade and walked with purpose. Jed wiped sweat from his brow, worried the glamour wasn't doing its job.

The wind blew.

Jed sneezed.

Shit.

The Angel picked up his pace and began running in Jed's direction. The shuffling sound got even louder as five of the dead broke onto the street and went after the Angel.

Get your copy of Etched in Darkness

www.ingramcontent.com/pod-product-compliance
Lightning Source LLC
Chambersburg PA
CBHW030830200726
48285CB00007B/2401